Memoirs of a Teenage Amnesiac

Memoirs of a Teenage Amnesiac

GABRIELLE ZEVIN

BLOOMSBURY

First published in Great Britain in 2007 by Bloomsbury Publishing Plc,
36 Soho Square, London, W1D 3QY

First published in the United States of America in 2007
by Farrar, Straus & Giroux, LLC

A CIP catalogue record of this book is available from the British Library

ISBN 978 0 7475 9165 8

All papers used by Bloomsbury Publishing are natural, recyclable
products made from wood grown in well-managed forests.
The manufacturing processes conform to the environmental
regulations of the country of origin.

Printed and bound in Great Britain by Clays Ltd, St Ives Plc

10 9 8 7 6 5 4 3 2 1

www.bloomsbury.com/GabrielleZevin

For my editor, Janine O'Malley,
on or about the occasion of her marriage

Above all, mine is a love story.

And like most love stories, this one involves chance, gravity, a dash of head trauma.

It began with a coin toss.

The coin came up tails; I was heads.

Had it gone my way, there might not be a story at all. Just a chapter or a sentence in a book whose greater theme had yet to be determined. Maybe this chapter would have had the faintest whisper of love about it, but maybe not.

Sometimes, a girl needs to lose.

I was

One

IF THINGS HAD BEEN DIFFERENT, I'D BE CALLED
Nataliya or Natasha, and I'd have a Russian accent and chapped lips
year round. Maybe I'd even be a street kid who'd trade you just about
anything for a pair of blue jeans. But I am not Nataliya or Natasha,
because at six months old I was delivered from Kratovo, Moscow
Oblast, to Brooklyn, New York. I don't remember the trip or ever
having lived in Russia at all. What I know about my orphanhood is
limited to what I've been told by my parents and then by what they
were told, which was sketchy at best: a week-old baby girl was found
in an empty typewriter case in the second-to-last pew of an Eastern
Orthodox Church. Was the case a clue to my biological father's pro-
fession? Did the church mean my birth mother was devout? I'll never
know, so I choose not to speculate. Besides, I hate orphan stories.
They're all the same, but most books are bursting with them anyway.
You start to think everyone in the whole world must be an orphan.

I can't remember a time when I didn't know I was adopted. There was never a dramatic "we have something to tell you" talk. My adoption was simply another fact, like having dark hair or no siblings. I knew I was adopted even before I knew what that truly meant. Understanding adoption requires a basic understanding of sex, something I would not have until third grade when Gina Papadakis brought her grandparents' disturbingly dog-eared copy of *The Joy of Sex* to school. She passed it around at lunch and while most everyone else was gagging with the realization that their parents had done *that* to make *them* (so much hair, and the people in the drawings were not one bit joyful . . .), I felt perfectly fine, even a little smug. I might be adopted, but at least my parents hadn't degraded themselves like that for my sake.

You're probably wondering why they didn't do it the old-fashioned way. Not that it's any of your business, but they tried for a while without getting anywhere. After about a year, Mom and Dad decided that, rather than invest about a billion dollars on fertility treatments that might not work anyway, it would be better to spend the money helping some sob story like me. This is why you are not, at the very moment, holding in your hands the inspiring true account of a Kratovan orphan called Nataliya, who, things being different, might be named Nancy or Naomi.

Truth is, I rarely think about any of this. I'm only telling you now because, in a way, I was born to be an amnesiac. I have always been required to fill in the blanks.

But I'm definitely getting ahead of myself.

When he heard about my (for lack of a better term) accident, my best friend, Will, who I'd completely forgotten at the time, wrote me a letter. (I didn't come across it immediately because he had slipped it inside the sleeve of a mix CD.) He had inherited a battered black typewriter from his great-uncle Desmond who'd supposedly been a war correspondent, though Will was unclear which war it had been. There was a dent on the carriage return that Will theorized might be from a ricocheting bullet. In any case, Will liked composing letters on the typewriter, even when it would have been much easier to send an e-mail or call a person on the phone. Incidentally, the boy wasn't antitechnology; he just had an appreciation for things other people had forgotten.

I should tell you that the following dispatch, while being the only record of the events leading up to my accident, does not really convey much of Will's personality. It was completely unlike him to be so formal, stiff, boring even. You do get some sense of him from his footnotes, but half of you probably won't bother with those anyway. I know I didn't. At the time, I felt about footnotes nearly the same way I did about orphan stories.

```
Chief:

The first thing you should know about me is
that I remember everything, and the second
thing is that I'm probably the most honest
person in the world. I realize that you can't
trust anyone who says that they're honest,
and knowing this, I wouldn't normally say
something like that about myself. I'm only
telling you now because it's something I feel
you should know.

In an attempt to make myself useful to you,
I have assembled a timeline of the events
```

leading up to your accident, which you may or
may not find helpful, but you will find
below.

6:36 p.m. Naomi Porter and William Landsman,
Co-editors of the national-award-winning[1]
Thomas Purdue Country Day School yearbook,
leave the offices of The Phoenix.[2]
6:45 p.m. Porter and Landsman arrive at the
student parking lot. Porter realizes that
they have left the camera back at the office.
6:46 p.m. Discussion[3] ensues regarding who
should have to return to the office to
retrieve the camera. Landsman suggests
settling the matter with a coin toss,[4] a
proposition which Porter accepts. Landsman
says that he will be heads, but Porter
states[5] that she should be heads. Landsman
concedes, as oft happens. Landsman flips the
coin, and Porter loses.
6:53 p.m. Landsman drives home; Porter
returns to The Phoenix.
7:02 p.m.[6] (approx.) Porter arrives at the

---

1. Honorable Mention, NSPA.
2. While school starts after Labor Day for mere mortals, it
starts in August for football players, marching band, and
us. And bird-watchers. We had been planning to photograph
the first meeting of the Tom Purdue Bird-watching Society
the next morn.
3. We often "discuss" things. Others might call this
"arguing."
4. Poses a series of interesting philosophical questions
which I am still pondering, but am not prepared to discuss
at this time.
5. Also "arguing."
6. Unfortunately, from this point forward, I have had to rely
on the reports of others, like your dad and that cat James.

Phoenix office where she retrieves the camera.
<u>7:05 p.m.</u> (approx.) Porter falls down the
exterior front steps at school. Porter
strikes head on bottom step, but manages to
hold on to the camera.[7] Porter is discovered
by one James Larkin.[8]

As Ⅲ mentioned to you, Ⅲ am always available
to answer any other questions as they might
arise.

Ⅲ remain your faithful servant,

William B.[9] Landsman

P.S. Apologies for the "Ⅲ" [i] key.
Hopefully, you've figured out by now that the
thing that resembles a trident is actually
the letter "Ⅲ." There's a defect in my
typewriter such that every time capital "i"
is pressed, "U" comes down with it.

---

7. The camera was an Oneiric 8000 G Pro, which we had just
purchased for $3,599.99 tax free plus shipping, using the
entire proceeds of last year's wrapping paper fundraiser.
The staff of The Phoenix thanks you.
8. Ⅲ don't know what he was doing there that day.
9. Ⅲ imagine you have also forgotten that the "B" stands
for Blake, although William Blake is probably my least
favorite poet and Ⅲ only feel fifty percent about him as an
artist. The woman responsible for the name, aka my mother,
will also be your AP English teacher, aka Mrs. Landsman.

Of course, I didn't remember any of this. Not the coin toss.
Not the camera. Certainly not my best friend, the veracious William
Blake Landsman.

The first thing I remembered was "that cat" James Larkin,

though I didn't even know his name at the time. And I didn't remember all of James, James proper. Just his voice, because my eyes were still closed and I guess you'd call me asleep. Or half-asleep, like when your alarm clock sounds and you manage to ignore it for a while. You hear the radio and the shower; you smell coffee and toast. You know you will wake; it's only a question of when, and of what or who will finally push you into day.

His voice was low and steady. I've always associated those types of voices with honesty, but I'm sure there are loads of low-pitched liars just waiting to take advantage of easy prey like me. Even semiconscious, I lapsed into my prejudices and decided to trust every word James said: "Sir, my name is James Larkin. Unfortunately her family is not here, but I am her boyfriend, and I am riding in this ambulance." I didn't hear anyone argue with him. His tone did not allow for discussion.

Someone took my hand, and I opened my eyes. It was him, though I didn't know his face.

"Hey there," he said softly, "welcome back."

I did not stop to consider where I had been that required welcoming. I did not even ask myself why I was in an ambulance with a boy who said he was my boyfriend but whom I did not readily recognize.

As ridiculous as this might seem, I tried to smile, but I doubt if he even saw. My attempt didn't last that long.

The pain came. The kind of pain for which there is no analogy; the kind of pain that allows for no other thought. The epicenter was concentrated in the area above my left eye, but it barely mattered; the waves through the rest of my head were almost worse. My brain felt too large for my skull. I felt like I needed to throw up, but I didn't.

Without my having to tell him, James asked, "Could someone please give her some drugs?"

An EMT shone a light in my eyes. "Not until she's seen a doctor, maybe even had a CT scan. But it's terrific news that she's already up. Just five more minutes, okay, Naomi?"

"Just five more minutes *until what*?" I asked, trying to sound patient. Until Christmas? Until my head exploded?

"Sorry. Until we're at the hospital," said the EMT.

At this point, the pain in my head was so strong that I wanted to weep. I probably would have, too, but it occurred to me that crying might actually make me feel worse.

"Are you positive she can't have any drugs?" James yelled.

"Distract her. Tell her a joke or something. We're almost there," was the EMT's annoying, unhelpful reply.

"I don't think that's gonna do it," James retorted.

"Laughter's the best medicine," said the EMT. I believe this may have been his idea of a joke, but it did nothing for my headache.

"Complete and utter . . ." James leaned in closer to me. He smelled like smoke and laundered sheets left to dry in the sun. ". . . bullshit, but would you like a joke anyway?" he asked.

I nodded. I really would have preferred drugs.

"Well, I can only think of one, and it's not that good. Certainly not analgesic good. So . . . okay, this man goes to a psychiatrist and says, 'My wife's insane. She thinks she's a chicken.' And the doctor goes, 'Well, why don't you just commit her?' And the man says—"

Just as he was about to reveal the punch line, a particularly impressive wave of pain pulsed through my head. My nails dug into James's palm, piercing his skin, making him bleed. I couldn't speak, so I tried to telegraph my apology with a look.

13

"No worries," James said, "I can take it." He winked at me.

In the emergency room, a doctor with eyes so bloodshot they made me tired just looking at them asked James how long I had been passed out, and he replied twenty-one minutes, he knew exactly. He'd seen it happen. "At Tom Purdue, there're these steps out front. One second, she's walking down them and the next, she's flying headfirst toward me, like a meteor."

"Is it strange that I don't remember that?" I asked.

"Nope," said the doctor. "Perfectly ordinary to forget incident-associated narrative for a time." She shined a light in my eyes, and I flinched.

At some point, another doctor and a nurse had joined the party, though I couldn't have told you when with any confidence. Nor can I recall much about them as individuals. They were an indistinct blur of pastel and white uniforms, like chalk doodles on a sidewalk in the rain.

The second doctor said that she had to ask me a couple of questions, general ones, not about the accident.

"Your full name?"

"Naomi Paige Porter."

"Where do you live?"

"Tarrytown, New York."

"Good, Naomi, good. What year is it?"

"Two thousand and . . . 2000, maybe?"

Even as I said it, I knew it wasn't right. Because if it was 2000, I would have been twelve, and I knew for sure I wasn't twelve. I didn't feel twelve. I felt . . . I couldn't say the exact number, but I just knew I felt older. Seventeen. Eighteen. My body didn't feel twelve. My mind didn't feel twelve either. And there was James, James proper—James looked at least seventeen, maybe older—and I felt the same age as him, the same as him. I looked from doctor to doctor to nurse: poker faces, every one.

One of the doctors said, "Okay, that's fine for now. Try not to worry." This made me worry, of course.

I decided that the best thing for me to do would be to go home and sleep it off. I tried to sit up in the gurney, which made my head throb even more intensely than it had been.

"Whoa, Naomi, where you going?" the nurse said. He and James gently pushed me back into a horizontal position.

The doctor repeated, "Try not to worry."

The other doctor paraphrased, "Really, you shouldn't worry."

As they walked across the ER to some other patient, I heard the doctors muttering to each other all sorts of worrisome phrases: "mild traumatic brain injury" and "specialist" and "CT scan" and "possible retrograde amnesia." I have a tendency to deal with things by not dealing with them at all, so instead of demanding that someone immediately tell me what was wrong, I just listened until I couldn't hear them anymore and then decided to concentrate on matters more tangible.

James always said how ugly he was, but I think he must have known that he wasn't. The only bad thing anyone could have said about him was that he was too skinny, but never mind that. Maybe because I couldn't seem to remember anything else, I felt like I needed to memorize every single thing about him. His fraying white dress shirt was open, so I could see that he was wearing a really old concert T-shirt—it was faded to the point that I couldn't even tell what the band was. His boxers were sticking out over his jeans, and I could make out they were a dark green plaid. His fingers were long and thin like the rest of him, and a few of them were smudged with black ink. His hair was damp with sweat, which made it even darker than usual. Around his neck was a single leather rope with a silver ring on it, and I wondered if the ring was mine. His collar had gotten half turned up. I noticed blood on his lapels.

"There's blood on your collar," I said.

"Um . . . it's yours." He laughed.

I laughed, too, even though it made my brain beat like a heart. "In the ambulance . . ." For whatever reason, the phrase *in the ambulance* embarrassed me, and I had to rephrase. "In the van, you said you were my boyfriend?"

"Hmm, I hadn't known you were listening to that." He had this funny smile on his face and he shook his head a couple of times, as if in conversation with himself. He let go of my hand and laid it on the gurney. "No," he said, "I just said you were my girlfriend so they would let me ride with you. I didn't want you to be alone."

This was disappointing news, to say the least.

There's a joke about amnesiacs, which always reminds me of meeting James. It's not exactly a joke, but more a "funny" slogan you'd wear on a T-shirt if you were a) an amnesiac, and b) extremely corny, and c) probably had issues in addition to amnesia, like low self-esteem or the need to give "too much information" or just plain bad taste in clothes. Okay, picture a really cheap, fifty-percent-polyester jersey with a white front and red sleeves. Now add the words "Hi, I'm an amnesiac. Have we met before?"

"You know something funny?" I said. "The first thing I thought about you was what an honest voice you had, and it turns out you were lying to me."

"No. Not to you. Only to some jerk in a uniform," he corrected. "If I'd been thinking at all, I would have said you were my sister. No one would have even questioned that."

"Except me. I don't have any siblings." I tried to make a joke of it. If given the choice, I preferred being his imaginary girlfriend to being his imaginary sister. "Are we friends, at least?"

"No, Naomi," James said with the same little smile, "can't say that we are."

"Why not?" He seemed like the kind of person it might be nice to be friends with.

"Maybe we ought to be" was all he replied.

It was and it wasn't a satisfactory answer, so I tried a different question. "Before, when you were shaking your head, what were you thinking?"

"You're really gonna ask me that?"

"You have to tell me. I might die, you know."

"I didn't take you for the manipulative kind."

I closed my eyes and pretended to pass out.

"Oh, all right, but that's awful low," he said with a resigned laugh. "I was wondering if I could get away with letting you think I was your boyfriend. And then I decided that would definitely be the wrong thing to do. It wouldn't be fair—you don't even know what year it is, for God's sake. A good relationship is not built on lies and all that crap.

"And well, I also wondered if it would be wrong to kiss you— not on the mouth, maybe on your forehead or hand—while I had the chance, while you were still thinking you were mine. And I decided that would be very, very wrong and probably uncomfortable later on. Plus, a girl like you probably does have a boyfriend—"

I interrupted. "You think?"

James nodded. "Definitely. I don't give a damn about him, but I didn't want to compromise you . . . or take advantage. I decided that if I ever kissed you, I'd want your permission. I'd want—"

At that moment, my dad came into the ER.

James had been leaning over the side of the gurney railing, but he stood up straight like a soldier to shake Dad's hand. "Sir," he said, "I'm James Larkin. I go to school with your daughter." But Dad pushed right past James to get to me, and James was left with his palm in the air, and I saw the four puncture wounds my nails had made from grabbing him so tight.

The doctors returned then, followed by a nurse, a specialist, and an orderly who began wheeling me away without even bothering to tell me where, and then I really had to throw up, and I didn't want James to have to watch that (I didn't want him to leave either), and somehow James slipped out without my seeing, which is something I would later find out he had a talent for.

Once I was admitted into a room, Dad passed the time by asking me if I was okay. "You okay, kid?"

"Yes, Dad."

Five seconds later, "Kiddo, are you okay?"

In an amazing display of restraint, I managed to reply *Yes, Dad* three more times even though I had no earthly idea if I was. On the fifth or sixth time, I finally just snapped, "Where's Mom?" She was better than Dad in these types of situations.

"In the city," he said. He kept pacing the room and looking up and down the hallway. "Christ, is anyone ever going to help us?"

"Is she working?" Mom was a photographer and she sometimes had to go into New York City for that.

"Working?" Dad repeated. His head was sticking out the door like a turtle, but he pulled it back inside so that he could look at me. "She's . . . She . . . Naomi, are you trying to worry me?"

"Dad, are you screwing with me?" Knowing my dad, this was not an unlikely scenario.

"*Screwing* with you?"

I assumed he hadn't liked my use of the word *screw*, though Dad was not normally the sort of parent who cared much about swearing. He always said that words were words and the only reason to ever eliminate any of them was if they were either hurtful (and you weren't meaning to be) or inexpressive. I figured that the anxiety of the situation must be getting to him, so I rephrased. "Sorry. *Playing* with me, whatever."

"Are you screwing with *me*?" Dad asked.

"So you can use *screw* and I can't? That doesn't seem fair," I protested.

"I don't give a damn if you use the word *screw*, Naomi. But is that what you're doing?"

"I'm not screwing with you! Just tell me where Mom is."

"In N.Y.C." It sounded like slow motion. EHNNNNN. WHYYYYY. SEEEEE. "New York—"

"City. Yes, I know what N.Y.C. stands for. But why?"

"She lives there. Since the divorce. You can't have forgotten that."

I'm sure you've already figured out that I had.

Everyone always says how much I look like her—my mom, I mean—which is ridiculous because she is half-Scottish and half-Japanese. We both have light blue eyes though, so I guess this accounts for the misunderstanding. No one ever says I look like Dad, which is ironic because he is actually part Russian. The rest of him is French, and all of him is Jewish, though he's not observant. All this makes everyone sound much more interesting than they are—my mom's really just a California girl, and my dad was born in D.C., and they met in college in New York City, where we used to live until I was eleven. If you're a wine-drinking type, you might have heard of them. They wrote a series of travel memoirs/coffee table books called *The Wandering Porters Do* . . . and then fill in the blank with the exotic locale of your choice, somewhere like Morocco or Tuscany. My mom took the pictures, and my dad wrote the text, except for the occasional footnote by Mom. Her footnotes were usually something mortifying, like "2. At an Edam cheese factory, Naomi vomited in an enormous wooden clog." Or "7. Naomi was particularly fond of the schnitzel." As for my contribution, I made a series of increasingly awkward appearances in their author photo on the back jacket flap above the caption "When not wandering, Cassandra Miles-Porter and Grant Porter live in New York with their daughter, Naomi."

That's what popped into my head when Dad said they were divorced—all those Wandering Porter books and me as a kid on the back flap. In a strange way, I didn't feel like their divorce was happening to me, certainly not the "me" in that moment, the person lying in the hospital bed. It was happening to that little girl on the book jackets. I felt sad for her, but nothing yet for myself.

"Did it just happen?" I asked.

"Did *what* just happen?"

"The divorce."

"It's been two years, eleven months, but we've been separated close to four years now," Dad said. Something in his tone told me he probably knew the precise number of days, too. Maybe even minutes and seconds. Dad was like that. "The doctors, they said you weren't sure of the year before, but . . . Well, do you think this is part of the same thing?"

I didn't answer him. For the first time, I allowed for the possibility that I had forgotten *everything* from the last four years.

I tried to remember the last thing I could remember. This turns out to be an incredibly difficult task because your brain is constantly making new memories. What came to mind was uselessly recent: my blood on James's collar.

I decided to make a more specific request of my brain. I tried to remember the last thing I could about my mother. What came to me was her "Sign of the Times" show, which was an exhibition of her photographs at a Brooklyn gallery. She picked me up on the last day of sixth grade, so that she could give me a private showing before anyone else got there. The show had consisted of her pictures of signs from around the country and the world: street, traffic, restaurant, township, movie theater, bathroom, signs that were painted over but you could still make them out, signs handmade by homeless people or hitchhikers, etc. Mom had this theory that you could tell everything about people (and civilization in general) from the kinds of signs they put up. For example, one of her favorite pictures was of a mostly rusted sign in front of a house somewhere in the backwoods.

The sign read NO DOGS NEGROS MEXICANS. She said that, regardless of the rust, it had communicated to her clear as anything "to take the picture quick and get the hell out of town." Most of her exhibit was more boring than that, though. As we were leaving, I told her I was proud of her because that's what my parents always said to me whenever they came to see a dance recital or attended a school open house. Mom replied that she was "proud of herself, too." I could remember her smiling just before she started to cry.

"So is Mom on her way, then?" I asked Dad.

"I didn't think you'd want her here."

I told him that she was my mother, so of course I wanted her.

"The thing is"—Dad cleared his throat before continuing—"I *have* called her, but since you haven't really spoken to each other for a while, it didn't seem right that she come." Dad furrowed his brow. I noticed that he had less hair on his head than my brain was telling me he ought to have. "Do you want me to call her back?"

I did. I longed for Mom in the most primitive way, but I didn't want to seem like a baby or not like myself, whatever that meant. And Mom and I not speaking? It seemed so unbelievable to me and like more than I could even begin to figure out in my current state. I needed time to think.

I told Dad that he didn't need to call Mom, and his brow unfurrowed a wrinkle or two. "Well, that's what I thought," he said.

About a minute later, Dad clapped his hands together before taking his pad and pencil out of his back pocket. He always carried them in case he should be inspired. "You should make a list of everything you don't remember," he said, holding the pencil out to me.

Although my dad writes mainly books for a living, what he loves writing most are lists. Groceries, books he's read, people he's angry at, the list goes on. If he could write lists for money instead of books, I think he'd be a happier person overall. I once said that to him, and he laughed before replying, "What do you think a table of contents is, kid? A book is just a very detailed and elaborate list."

My father is one of those people who believe that anything can be accomplished, the ills of the world cured, so long as it's written down and assigned a number. Maybe it's genetic, because I am most definitely not one of those people.

"So how about it?" Dad was still holding the pencil out to me.

"If I can't remember it in the first place, how'll I remember to put it on the list?" I asked. It was the most absurd thing in a day of absurd things, as ridiculous as asking a person who has lost her keys where she had last seen them.

"Oh. Good point." Dad tapped on his head with his pencil. "Brain's still working better than your old man's, I see. How about, as you hear things you don't remember, you tell me, and I'll write them down for you?"

I shrugged. At least it would keep Dad occupied.

"Things Naomi has forgotten," he said as he wrote. "Number one, Cass's and my divorce." He held up the paper to show me. "Just seeing it written down, doesn't that make it all so much less frightening?"

It didn't.

"Number two," he continued. "Everything after Cass's and my divorce. So that would be 2001, right?"

"I don't know." I knew Dad was trying to be helpful, but he was really starting to annoy the crap out of me.

"Number ten. Your boyfriend, I'm assuming?"

"I have a boyfriend?" I thought of what James had said.

Dad looked at me. "Ace. He's still away at tennis camp." He made a note.

My dad was up to nineteen ("Driver's Ed? No. Driving? Maybe.") when a nurse came into the room to wheel me away for my first of many tests. I remember feeling relieved that I didn't have to hear twenty.

I was in the hospital for three more nights. A rotating coven of evil nurses would wake me up every three hours or so by shining a flashlight in my eyes. This is what they do when you've had a head trauma: all you want to do is sleep, and no one will let you. Besides not sleeping, the rest of my time was occupied with taking boring tests, ignoring my father's incessant list-making, and wondering if James Larkin might take it upon himself to visit.

He didn't.

My first visitor was William Landsman. Visiting hours began at eleven o'clock on Fridays, and Will showed up at 10:54. My dad had gone outside to make a few phone calls, so there was no one around to even tell me who this teenage boy in the maroon smoking jacket was. "Nice save, Chief!" Will said as he entered the room.

I asked him what he meant, and he explained about my rescue of the yearbook camera. "Not a scratch on it. Really going above and beyond the call of duty there," he added.

Despite his questionable clothing choices, Will was not the least bit fussy or wimpy. When I asked him about the jacket, he claimed to wear it ironically, "as a way to entertain myself in the face of the daily monotony of school uniforms." He was compactly built, about my height (five feet seven inches), but solid-looking. He had wavy chestnut hair and dark blue eyes, sapphire or cerulean, a deeper shade than either mine or my mother's. His eyelashes were very long and looked as if they had been coated with mascara even though they hadn't been. On that day he had light dark circles under his eyes, and his cheeks were flushed. If he seemed loud or cavalier about my condition, I suspect now that it was a way of masking his concern for me. In any case, I liked him immediately. He felt comfortable and broken-in like favorite jeans. It probably goes without saying that James had had the opposite effect on me in the brief time that I had known him.

"Are you Ace?" I asked, remembering what Dad had said about my having a boyfriend.

Will removed his black rectangular-framed glasses and wiped them on his pants. I would later learn that removing his glasses was something Will did when embarrassed, as if not seeing something clearly could in some way distance him from an awkward situation. "No, I most definitely am not," he said. "Ace's about six inches taller than me. And also, he's your boyfriend." A second later, Will's eyes flashed something mischievous. "Okay, so this is deeply wrong. I want it on the record that you are acknowledging that this is deeply wrong before I even say it."

"Fine. It's wrong," I said.

"Deeply—"

"*Deeply* wrong."

"Good." Will nodded. "I feel so much better that you don't re-member *him* either. By the by, your man's a dolt not to come."

"Dolt?" Who used *dolt*?

"Tool. No offense."

"Leave. Right now," I said in a mock stern tone. "You go too far insulting Ace . . . What's his last name?"

"Zuckerman."

"Right. Zuckerman. Yeah, I'm really outraged about you insulting the boyfriend I don't remember anyway."

"You might be later and if that's the case, I take it all back. Visiting hours only started a minute ago, so he'll probably still come," Will said, by way of encouragement I suppose.

"Dad said he was still at tennis camp."

"If it were my girlfriend, I would have come back from tennis camp."

"Who's your girlfriend?" I asked.

"I don't have one. I was speaking hypothetically." Will chuckled and then stuck out his hand for me to shake. "Introductions are in order. I am William Landsman, the Co-editor of *The Phoenix*. Incidentally, you're the other Co-editor. Your dad said you might have forgotten some things, but I didn't think it was possible *I* might be one of them."

"Are you *that* memorable?"

"Pretty much. Yes." He nodded decisively.

"And humble." I didn't need to remember him to know exactly how to tease him.

"And also your best friend, if you haven't already figured it out." Will cleaned his glasses again.

"Really? My best friend wears a smoking jacket?" I nodded. "That's very interesting."

"It's *ironic*. Seriously though, you can ask me anything. Honest to God, Chief, I know everything about you."

I looked in his eyes, and I decided to trust him. "How does my face look?" Since they'd stitched up my forehead, I'd been basically trying to avoid my reflection.

He examined me from both sides and then from the front. "A little swollen around your left eye and cheekbone, but most of it's covered by the tape and gauze."

"Look under the gauze, will you?"

"Chief, I am not looking under the gauze for you! It's completely unsanitary and probably against the rules! Do you want me to get kicked out of here and not be able to visit you?"

"I want a report before I have to see it for myself. I want to know if I'm, like, disfigured." I tried to say this casually, but I was scared. "Please, Will, it's important."

Will sighed heavily before grumbling, "I said I'd tell you anything, not that I'd do anything. I want it on the record that I, William Landsman, did not want to do this, and am furthermore not trained for medical procedures." He went into my room's doll house W.C. and washed his hands before returning to my bedside. He placed his left hand gently on the right side of my face before using his right hand to slowly remove a section of surgical tape from the left side near my hairline. "Tell me if I'm hurting you. Even a little." I nodded.

When one of my hairs got pulled in the tape, I winced what I thought was imperceptibly, and Will stopped. "Am I hurting you?"

I shook my head. "Go on."

Ten seconds later he had removed enough of the tape so that he could lift up the gauze and look under it. "There are nine stitches, and a raised knob right below that, probably the size of a brussels sprout, and a larger bruise spread out across your forehead. None of it looks permanent. You'll probably have a tiny scar from the stitches." He refastened the gauze as delicately as he had removed it. "You're still insanely, unfairly, torturously beautiful, and that's the last I'm gonna say about it, Chief."

"Thank you," I said.

"You are welcome," he said jauntily. "Glad to be of service." He tipped an imaginary hat. "Don't think I'm unaware that you were really just fishing for compliments."

"Yup, you see right through me," I said.

Will leaned in close and whispered, "Come on, admit it. You really do remember me. All this amnesia crap is so you can get a break from *The Phoenix*."

"How'd you know? I just didn't want to hurt your feelings, Landsman."

"That's real considerate of you."

"So, what's my boyfriend like?" I asked him.

"Let's see. Ace Zuckerman is an awfully good tennis player."

"You're saying you don't like him."

"As he's not my boyfriend, I don't think I'm technically required to, Chief."

"What about James Larkin?"

"James Larkin. Larkin comma James. Yeah, we haven't really met him yet. He's new this year, which is unusual for a senior. I think he might have gotten kicked out of his last school or something."

"A delinquent?" That was interesting . . .

Will shrugged. "I only met him this morning when he dropped

off the camera at *The Phoenix* and he was polite as anything. FYI, the kid is nothing like Ace Zuckerman." He paused. "Or me." He reached into his messenger bag and pulled out his laptop. "You have your headphones with you, right?"

I shook my head. "I'm not sure."

"You always do. Where's your bag?"

I pointed to the closet in the corner of the room. Will opened the door and started digging through my backpack, which probably should have bothered me, but it didn't. It seemed like someone else's bag anyway. He pulled out an iPod, presumably mine, then plugged it into his laptop. "When I heard from your dad, I decided to make you a mix. Don't worry. I burned it for you, too." He handed me a CD and a playlist entitled *Songs for a Teenage Amnesiac*, Vol. I. "It's not one of my best. Some of the selections are a little broad," he continued, "but I was under time constraints. I promise that Volume II will be better, as it is with, for example, the second record of the Beatles' *White Album* or the Godfather movies."

Will handed me my headphones and put away his laptop. He started speaking really fast. "It's hard to make a good mix. You don't want anything too cliché, but you don't want to make the songs too obscure either. Plus, you can only fit about nineteen tracks on a CD, and you want each one to say something different, and you want a balance of slow and fast songs, and then there's the added pressure of making sure each track organically leads to the next. Plus, you've got to know the person for whom the mix is intended really well. For example, on yours each of the songs means something. Like the first one is sort of how we met freshman year. I thought it might jog your memory."

I read the CD liner. " 'Fight Test,' the Flaming Lips?"

29

"Yeah, I was on the fence between that and 'Yoshimi Battles the Pink Robots, Part I.' And also 'To Whom It May Concern' by John Wesley Harding. I eliminated that one first 'cause I had another of his songs I wanted to use and it's bad form to duplicate artists. The one I used instead is called 'Song I Wrote Myself in the Future,' and it's the next to last track."

I was about to ask him how we *had* met, but I was interrupted by the arrival of someone who made me forget the mix and William Landsman for the time being.

"Hi, Mrs. Miles," Will said to my mother.

"Hello there," she replied uncertainly.

Will laughed. "We've never met before, but I've seen your picture. I'm William Landsman, Will."

"Could we have a moment alone?" my mother asked Will.

Will looked at me. "You'll be okay?"

I nodded.

"I should be getting back to yearbook anyway," Will said.

"There's yearbook in the summer?" I asked.

"It never quits." He took my hand in his and shook it rather formally. "I'll call you," he promised. "Don't forget to charge up your cell phone."

After Will closed the door, neither my mother nor I spoke.

My mother is beautiful, and since I'm adopted you can know I'm not saying that as some sort of backhanded way of telling you how pretty I am. Besides, everyone says so. And she isn't beautiful in any of the clichéd ways. She's not tall and skinny and blond with big boobs or something. She's little and curvy with wavy light brown hair halfway down her back and almond-shaped ice blue eyes. It felt like I hadn't seen her in forever. I almost started to cry, but something kept me from doing it.

Mom, however, did not hold back. She burst into tears almost as soon as she got to my bedside. "I told myself I wasn't going to do that," she said. She mock-slapped herself across the face before taking my hand.

"Where were you?" I asked.

"Your dad told me not to come, that you didn't want me. But how could I not come?" She looked at my face. "Your poor head." She ever so gently stroked my brow, and then she leaned over to hug me. I pulled away. I needed to know a few things first.

"You and Dad are divorced."

She nodded.

"But why?"

Dad came into the room then. His voice was hard as bricks. "Yes, tell her, Cass."

"I can explain." Mom's eyes started to tear again. "You were twelve when I ran into Nigel. It was just by chance."

"Who's Nigel?"

"Her high school boyfriend," Dad answered for her.

"Just by chance," Mom repeated. "I was waiting for the subway, and it was the most random thing in the whole—"

I told her that I didn't want a story, only facts.

"I . . ." she began again. "This is so hard."

I told her that I didn't want adjectives and adverbs, only nouns and verbs. I asked her if she could handle that. She nodded and cleared her throat.

"I had an affair," she said.

"I got pregnant," she said.

"Your dad and I divorced," she said.

"I married Nigel and moved back to the city."

"You have a three-year-old sister."

"Sister?" It was a foreign word on my tongue, gibberish. Sisters were something other people had, like mono or ponies.

"But I thought you couldn't have children," I said.

Dad whispered to my mother something about how he had been trying to break this to me slowly, how I had already been through *a lot*. He had never mentioned my sister or Mom's pregnancy, which seemed odd, especially when you consider all his list-making. I wondered what else he'd been holding back.

"Sister?" I repeated. It felt even more made up the second time.

"Yes. Her name is Chloe."

"Are we close?" I asked.

"No," Mom said. "You refuse to see her."

I couldn't think of anything to say.

"It's probably a lot to hear all at once," Dad said.

"How are you feeling, cupcake?" Her voice was high and whispery. She sounded like she was floating away.

How did I feel? "About what? Which part?"

"About everything I've just told you, I suppose."

What I felt was that all of these were very good reasons for us not to be speaking. It was one thing for Mom and Dad to have gotten divorced, but for Mom to get together with her high school boyfriend and have an affair and a daughter and a whole new family . . . "I feel like"—her eyes were wide and expectant—"I honestly feel repulsed. I honestly feel like you're a slut."

"Naomi," Dad said.

"What?" I asked. "She is. Women who cheat on their husbands and get pregnant are sluts. Why don't you add that one to your list, Dad?"

Mom stood up and started backing away from my bed, not quite able to look me in the eye. "I understand," she said, "I understand. I understand." Finally, Dad said that he thought she should go, which was funny because she seemed to be heading in that direction already.

"What happened to the Wandering Porters?" I asked after Mom had left.

"They wander no more." Dad tried to make a joke out of it. "The last book was Iceland. Do you remember that summer we went to Iceland?"

I did. We had left right after Mom's show, which may have even made it my last memory. I was twelve, and it had pretty much been fifty degrees all summer long, the coldest summer of my life. My mom and I used to say that it was the summer without any summer.

"What do you do now?" I asked.

"Your mom still takes pictures. I still write books. We just don't do it together. And the Wandering Porters are still in print mostly."

"What are your new books about?"

"Um . . . well, the last one was about . . . I'm not good at describing. It was about lots of things really," Dad said. "But the jacket copy said it was about 'the end of my marriage as seen through the prism of larger world events.' "

I interpreted. "It's about the divorce?"

"Basically. You could say that. Yes."

I asked him if I had liked it. He said that I hadn't even read it, but that the reviews had been pretty decent.

"Maybe I should read it now?" I said. "If my memory doesn't come back."

"Yeah, you could just skip through the parts about the Middle East," Dad suggested. "There's quite a bit about that, too. Not that you shouldn't be informed, but even I think it gets a little dry. Naomi, are you crying?"

I guess I was. "I'm sorry," I said. I turned onto my side, away from Dad. I didn't want him to watch me cry. In all likelihood, the reason he hadn't already told me about Mom and Chloe was because he hadn't wanted to discuss it himself.

Whenever Dad said anything serious, he would usually undercut it with a joke. That was his style. When he and my mom used to throw parties, he always had a funny story and could make everyone else laugh. My dad certainly wasn't what anyone would call shy, and yet he was. By himself, he was always a bit stingy with saying certain things. Like, he rarely said "I love you." I knew that he did love me. He just didn't say it a whole lot. My mom was the one with all the "I love you's." But I understood what Dad was like because I was like that, too. This was why I couldn't look at him.

"Why are you crying, kiddo? Is it your head?"

The doctors had told us that people with head injuries could be emotional, but it wasn't that. It was just . . . everything.

"It wasn't entirely your mother's fault. Mainly hers, but . . ." Dad laughed. "I'm kidding. Mostly."

I felt so alone.

"What is it? Please, tell your old man."

"I feel like an orphan." I was sobbing to the point that Dad couldn't understand me the first time and I had to repeat myself. "I'm an orphan."

It probably won't make any sense, but it was like my mother was less my mother than she had been before. Or maybe that I was less her child now that she had a new one. I was a vestigial daughter: an obsolete girl with an obsolete brain and an obsolete heart. I could hear my dad's breathing, but he didn't say anything and I still couldn't bear to look at him. I closed my eyes.

"Naomi?" Dad said after a while. "Are you sleeping?"

I kept my eyes closed and let him think that I was.

He kissed me on my forehead. "I'll never leave you, kid." He wouldn't have said this if he'd thought I was awake.

Two

BY MONDAY MORNING, THE DOCTORS HAD DETER-
mined that I couldn't remember most things after sixth grade, which
I'd pretty much known since that first conversation with Dad, and
they sent me home.

No one knew anything really. I was a bona fide medical mystery.
In their genius opinion, the head trauma wasn't severe enough to
have caused the kind of amnesia I had, so they said I was probably
repressing, or some such crap. Call me crazy, but I'm pretty sure it was
the fall down the stairs.

They said my memory might come back or it might not. And in
any case, we should all act as if it wasn't going to. There wasn't anything to be done anyway. In a couple of weeks, there would be more
pictures of my brain that probably wouldn't show anything. Therapy,
maybe.

"Rest," they said.

"And then?"

"Resume 'normal' life as much as possible," they said. "Go back to school when you're ready."

"Maybe it'll help you remember," they said. "But then again, maybe it won't."

"The human brain is mysterious," they said.

"Good luck to you," they said, handing me a sample-size bottle of Excedrin and an excuse note from gym; and Dad, a bill as thick as a *National Geographic*.

I scanned the hospital parking lot for our car, which in my last recollection had been a silver SUV (Mom's) or a red truck (Dad's). I didn't see either. "Dad, you think it's a bad sign that I don't know which car is ours?"

"I don't believe in signs," Dad said as he pointed to a compact white vehicle that was wedged between two other compact white vehicles.

"You're joking. You loved that truck!"

Dad muttered something about the new one being more fuel-efficient. "It's covered in the memoir," he added.

It was, though I wouldn't find this out for many months. He wrote about the truck on page ninety-eight of his book. He claimed to have sold it because it reminded him of Mom. He didn't mention a thing about fuel efficiency. It was funny how Dad was more honest in a book that anyone in the world could pick up and read than he could be talking to me. Or maybe it was sad. One or the other. Sometimes it's hard to tell.

I got into the passenger's seat and put on my seatbelt. Just as we were pulling away, Dad's cell phone rang, and he asked me did I mind if he took it. I said it was fine; after the doctors' near constant interrogation, I appreciated not talking.

"Yes. Hello. Me too. I've been meaning to call you . . ." Dad said stiffly to someone. He seemed embarrassed to be talking in front of me.

"Who is it?" I whispered.

"No one. Work," he mouthed to me. He rolled his eyes and slipped on a headset.

I decided I'd misread his tone and turned my concentration to the view outside. The trees were still green, but you could feel that summer was over. It made me think of a day I could remember, and how it had definitely been summer then. I didn't necessarily remember the trees, but I remembered the air that day. It had that fresh-cut-lawn smell, where it feels like all of nature is just *sighing* with relief. My parents and I had left for Iceland about a week later.

I wondered if Mom was having her affair even then. She must have been. She had said that her daughter was already three. My mother's daughter. My sister. I couldn't think about that yet.

Out the car window Tarrytown looked familiar enough. I noticed a new subdivision of houses and a new McDonald's. The place where they used to sell apple cider and doughnuts had been torn down. But basically, nothing much had changed, and this was reassuring.

All of a sudden, Dad turned onto a street I didn't recognize. Even though Dad was still on the phone, I asked him where we were going.

Dad hung up before answering. "We moved," he said simply. "I should have mentioned it before, but there were so many things. I'll add it to the list when we get home. We're almost there."

His list was turning out to be a complete waste.

Dad informed me that they had sold our house after the divorce. He had bought a different house about a half mile from our old one. He mentioned that the new house was "larger" (why we needed a larger house when fewer people lived in it was beyond me) and "closer to school" and "besides, we hadn't lived all that long in the other house anyway, not like Brooklyn."

The new house was much more modern than our old house had been. The back wall looked like it was made entirely from glass, and it was incredibly drafty inside. Our old house had been two stories with all these strangely shaped rooms and narrow flights of stairs. I think it had been built in 1803 or something. The new house was, well, new. It was on one level, and seemed more, I guess you might say, organized, if you were being kind. Sterile, if you weren't.

There were a few artifacts from the old house, but not many. At a glance I recognized a clay planter in front of the fireplace, a small braided rug near the laundry room, a cast-iron umbrella stand. They all looked awkward and out of place, like orphans.

"What do you think?" Dad smiled. I could tell he was proud of his house.

I didn't want to hurt his feelings, so I told him it was nice. Truly, there was nothing much to say. It was all very beige. The sofa was beige. The stain on the wood floor was beige. The walls were beige. What in the world can you say about beige?

To Mom, any reasonably flat or bare surface was a potential canvas, and she had always been painting and changing the colors of our walls. Our house smelled of paint, but also of all her other projects.

Like melted crayons and clay and weird incense and glue and newsprint. Like people lived there and things were happening there. Like home. This new house smelled like . . . synthetic citrus. "Dad, what's with the weird orange scent?"

"Just something the housekeeper uses. I didn't like it at first, but now I'm kind of used to it. It's organic." Dad sighed and then he clapped his hands together. "Okay, I assume you'll be wanting the official grand tour."

"Could we do it after lunch maybe?" I told Dad I was really tired, and he led me down the hall to "my room."

"Look at all familiar?" he asked.

Unlike the rest of the house, my room did share some similarities with the bedroom I remembered. The furniture, for one, was exactly the same. I practically wanted to hug my wicker dresser or, like, give my desk chair a massage.

I told Dad I wanted to be alone. He had just been standing there, and I sensed he needed to be told to leave. Dad nodded and said that he had some work to do, but that his office was down the hall if I wanted him.

"Oh hey, you'll need this!" Dad called just as he was about to go. He took the list out of his pocket. It was on five sheets of paper and one hundred eighty-six items long.

"It was lonesome here without you, kid," he said. He kissed me on the forehead to the right of my injuries. I closed the door behind him, and then I went to sleep.

Dad woke me for lunch and again for dinner, but the meals made no impression. I didn't really wake until around eight that night. I was alone for the first time in what felt like years, but had really been almost no time at all.

At the hospital I had basically avoided mirrors. It was easy. I just slipped past them, holding my breath as if there were a ghost in the room.

Partially I think it was because I didn't want to see my injuries. It probably sounds like vanity, but it wasn't. In my opinion, wounds are like water set to boil—they heal best left unwatched.

But every now and again I would accidentally catch a glimpse of myself. In a glass on my food tray, in the lenses of a doctor's spectacles, in the window at night before all the lights were turned out. For a moment, I would not even realize who I was looking at, and, instinctively, I would turn away. It is rude to stare at strangers and that is what I was to myself. I did not know the girl in the glass nor did she know me.

Now that I was finally alone, I felt braver. I decided that it was time to reacquaint myself with myself. The meeting couldn't be put off any longer.

The first thing I did was remove all my clothes and examine my body in the mirrored closet door.

It was what I had been expecting. Even though I had lost four years of memories, I had never actually thought that I was twelve. I'm not saying that it's like this for other people, but this is how it was for me. I instinctively knew I was older. And although my body was surprising in certain ways, it looked more or less how I felt inside, so it was okay.

My face was a bit more shocking to me, and not because of my injuries either—Will's description had been accurate on that front, and the whole mess was already changing colors, which I interpreted as healing. My face was strange because it looked like someone I knew, a cousin maybe, but not me. My hair was about the same length, halfway down my back, but it might have been highlighted, I wasn't sure. My jaw was narrower; my nose, sharper.

"Hello," I greeted myself. "I'm Naomi." The girl in the mirror didn't seem convinced.

"Anything you have to say for yourself?" I asked.

She stared at me blankly and said nothing.

I decided that mirrors were completely useless.

I found a T-shirt in my bureau and put it on.

I opened my closet door. The person who lived in my room (for I could not quite think of *her* as *me* yet) was incredibly organized. It was as if she had been preparing for just such an occasion.

I looked at my clothes. Several school uniforms: dark gray wool kilts, white dress shirts, maroon ties, various hoodies, and V-neck sweaters. Gym clothes. Tennis whites. All of it neatly pressed, folded, or hung. In a zipped garment bag was a black velvet dress for a formal I could not recall having attended. I decided to put it on, just to see what it looked like. The dress was a little tight around my breasts. Evidently, I had grown since I had last worn it. I didn't bother zipping it all the way up.

I ran my hands along my hips. The fabric was silky and plush.

I wondered if I had worn my hair up or down. I wondered if I had liked how I looked on that night and what my date had thought of me, if he'd said I was the most beautiful girl in the world. I wondered who my date had been, if it had been that Ace guy or someone else. I wondered if I had really liked the person or if I'd just gone to have someone to go with. I wondered if he had brought me a corsage and, if he had, what kind it had been. Had he known that I don't like roses? And if he'd brought roses, had I had to pretend to like them so that I wouldn't hurt his feelings? Maybe I hadn't gone with a boy at all? Maybe I'd just gone with a group of girls? Or a group of friends. Did I even have a group of friends?

Maybe I'd worn that dress somewhere else entirely? I wondered . . .

On the bookshelf under my window were four school yearbooks, one for each year beginning with seventh grade. I flipped through the books, but they didn't really tell me much. Teams competed in sports. Sometimes they won, and other times they lost. Some kids joined clubs; others didn't. Some got taller. Some got smarter; a few got dumber and, either way, most managed to graduate. All yearbooks told the same story anyway.

I read through every single signature of every single one: *Have a great summer. Don't forget me. Keep in touch.* I wondered why anyone bothered signing at all. The only interesting signature was Will's, and it wasn't really a signature. On the inside back cover of both my ninth- and tenth-grade books, he had drawn a very neat box around the perimeter. Above both boxes were the words "This page is reserved for William B. Landsman to do with what he will." He hadn't yet used it.

I wondered . . .

When I looked in the index of my most recent yearbook (tenth grade) under my name, I found only three mentions. The first was my class photo. That year, my hair looked very light on top, maybe blond, though I couldn't truly tell. All the underclassman portraits were black-and-white, so when I say my hair was blond, really what it looked was light gray. The second was the varsity tennis team photo. I wasn't even in that one, though—it just had my name and the caption "Not Pictured." I wondered what I had been doing instead. The third mention was on the yearbook masthead. I had been photo editor, which might have explained why I wasn't in any of the pictures.

It had always been the same with Mom—both in the Wandering Porter books and in our family albums. Because she was a photographer, she was never in the pictures, and whenever anyone tried to take her picture, she would get really uncomfortable. I put the yearbooks back on their shelf. Maybe I was like my mother, the girl behind the camera?

I wondered . . .

I went through the drawers of my nightstand. The most interesting thing I found was a plastic compact containing birth control pills, which meant I was either a) having sex with someone (!?!), or b) on the pill for some other reason. The second most interesting thing I found was a leather diary. This might have beat the birth control pills for the official title of Most Interesting Thing in Naomi's Nightstand, had it not been a *food diary* detailing every single thing I'd eaten for the last six months. Sample entry:

> August 4
> 1 Bagel with Cream Cheese, 350 calories
> 18 Mini Pretzels, 150 Calories
> 2 Diet Cokes, 0 Calories
> 1 Banana, 90 Calories
> 7 Reese's Pieces, 28 Calories
>
> GRAND TOTAL
> 618 Calories ☺

Every entry after that was the same way. Page after page of it. Sometimes there would be a ☹ if I thought I had eaten too much, or a ☺ if I was neither here nor there about my eating for the day. It went all the way until the day before my injury. I tried to toss the useless artifact in the trash, but I missed. I felt disgusted. I mean, really, what sort of person keeps a food diary?

I wondered if the former Naomi Porter had been, in all likelihood, a complete and total jerk, someone that I probably wouldn't have even wanted to know.

I wondered . . .

I went through my backpack. I suppose I could have done this at the hospital, but I never had. I looked at my driver's license. It had been issued nine months prior on my sixteenth birthday. I was wearing my school uniform, and in the picture I was smiling so big you could see that I still had braces. I ran my tongue over my teeth—smooth and no metal. Orthodontia—one thing I could be glad to have forgotten. As I returned the license to my backpack, I wondered if I still knew how to drive.

Also in my bag was my cell phone, which was dead, so I plugged it into the charger and turned it on.

I wanted to call someone, but I didn't know who, so I started scrolling through all the numbers in the address book. I didn't recognize about half the names. I thought about calling Will—maybe he would know about the birth control pills?—but I decided against it. Even if he was my "best friend," he was still a boy and I didn't want to ask him about that sort of thing.

Suddenly, I wanted to call my mom. Not because I thought she would know about the pills, I just missed her. I missed her like a reflex, even though I knew that it was just some trick of my undependable brain. Some stupid, vestigial part. The way humans have appendixes, even though they're pointless and mainly just a pain in the butt and people never even think about them unless they have to have them removed.

I didn't really want to talk to her, but I picked up the phone and dialed anyway. Of course I made sure to block the number in case she had caller ID or something. I knew I'd probably hang up, but I needed to hear her voice. Even if it was just her saying "Hello, who is this?" or breathing.

"Hi there," squeaked a precocious little voice, "you are speaking to Chloe Fusakawa, and I have just learned how to answer the phone."

This was my sister. I hadn't been prepared for that, and for a second, I couldn't speak.

"Helloooooooo . . . Is anyone there?"

"It's Nomi," I managed to say.

She giggled. "No me. No me is a funny name. It sounds like nobody. Hi, Nobody. Do you like to read?"

"Yes."

"Have you read *Goodnight Moon*?"

"Yes." My mother had read it to me when I was little.

"That is my seventh favorite book. It used to be fifth, but it is now too easy. It's still good. They have your name in it. There is a part that goes 'Goodnight, Nobody,' and this is my second favorite part of my seventh favorite book."

I heard my mother's familiar voice in the background. "Is someone on the phone, Chloe?"

"It's Nobody!" Chloe yelled.

"Then hang up the phone, sweetie! It's time for your bath!"

"I have to go now," Chloe said. "Bye-bye, Nobody. Call again, 'kay?"

"Okay."

I hung up the phone and felt lonelier than ever.

All I wanted to do was sleep.

Which was what I did.

For about a week, maybe two.

It was easy to lose track of time.

Three

I WOKE SUDDENLY: THREE SHARP TAPS ON MY window. I was startled because my old bedroom had been on the second floor. In other words, no one could knock on the window unless they had superpowers, like the ability to fly.

I sat up in bed and pulled back the curtain. It was dark outside, but I could still recognize Ace Zuckerman. I had seen his picture in my wallet and on my desk and in the yearbook and other places, too. In the flesh, though, he looked about as opposite of James as it gets. The contrast between my "boyfriend" and my "pretend boyfriend" was almost comical.

Ace was wearing jeans, like James had been, and a warm-up jacket. On Ace, though, everything was really filled out. I didn't have to see it to know that underneath his jacket was certainly not a faded concert T-shirt. Ace's hair was light brown and sort of shaggy. He was muscular. And handsome, I suppose, though in an almost cartoonish way. Everything about him seemed too broad, too big. If someone had asked me right at that moment, I would have said, "Definitely not my type."

I opened the window, and he swung himself over the frame. He moved like an athlete, and he knew to throw his legs way out in front of him so they wouldn't hit the bookshelf under my window. The casual grace of his movements alerted me to the fact that he had entered my room that way many times before.

The first thing he did was kiss me. On the lips. And he didn't ask my permission either.

I couldn't recall him ever having kissed me before.

I actually couldn't recall *anyone* ever having kissed me before.

So, in a way, this was my first kiss.

He tasted like Gatorade (could have been worse I suppose), and his tongue was dull, directionless, and too much in my mouth. The nicest thing I can say about it was that it ended quickly.

He pulled away, but was still sitting on the side of the bed. "You really don't remember me, do you?"

"No, but I know who you are. You're my . . ." He looked at me hopefully, but I couldn't bring myself to say the word. "My . . ."

"Boyfriend," he finished. "Ace."

"Yes, my boyfriend."

"I'm sorry I didn't come earlier. It's just . . . I was away at tennis camp. I'm a counselor this year and . . ."

"Really, you play tennis? I do, too." I was just making conversation. I already knew that, of course.

"I know you do. That's how we met. You're good." All of a sudden, he smacked himself in the head, and the violence of it actually scared me. "I choked! I should have left camp early. I should have come!"

"It's fine, Al."

"The name's Ace," he whispered.

"I know that." I had no idea why I had called him Al. I knew his name, but I think I had been momentarily stunned by the self-flagellation.

He cleared his throat and changed the subject. "Here, I brought you something. I was at the camp Pro Shop, and I guess these reminded me of you." He took a pair of white terry cloth tennis wristbands out of his pocket.

I wondered what about me screamed *tennis sweatbands* to him. Had he meant them as a joke? I could tell by his mouth—a thin pink line of determined patience and anticipation—that he hadn't.

It certainly wasn't the most romantic gift ever, but you know, it was obvious the guy meant well, so I put the wristbands on.

"Looks nice," he said. "With your, um, pajamas."

I walked over to my closet mirror under the pretense of looking at my wristbands, but what I actually did was study Ace's reflection. I was trying to figure him out, and sometimes it's easier to do that when people don't know that you're looking at them. I watched him watching me. His eyes were tired, and he seemed pleased that I was wearing his gift. Maybe there was something wistful in his look, maybe it was the pills in my drawer (*duh*), but all of a sudden I realized that I was probably having sex with him. I also decided I didn't want to have that conversation *just yet*; it was difficult to predict where such a conversation might lead.

Instead, I turned away from the mirror, walked across my bedroom, and kissed him again, like maybe I could figure things out that way. His lips were soft, but his chin was sandpaper against my face, even though I hadn't seen any hair on it. After about ten seconds, which seemed like way too many, I pulled back. "So, thanks for these," I said. I didn't know how to break it to Ace that the doctors said I had to refrain from all sports for the next couple of months. "Do I, um, play much tennis this time of year?"

"You start practicing in early spring," he reported. "But you'll definitely get a lot of use out of them then. I was thinking long-term, I guess.

"I'm sorry," he said, "about the way I came in. I shouldn't have kissed you. I should have let you kiss me. I definitely shouldn't have used tongue. I, well, I panicked. I choked. I'm not usually a choker. Not on the courts. Not off them either."

I told him it was okay, that these were confusing times or something like that. Then I said I had a headache, and he took that as his cue to leave the same way he'd come.

I closed the curtains. I was about to take off the wristbands when Dad knocked softly at the door. "Oh, you're awake? I was just planning to slip out." I looked at the clock; it was already 9:30 p.m.

"Where?" I asked.

"Just to get some coffee. We're all out, and I'm probably going to be up late working," he said. "Do you need anything?"

I told him that I didn't.

"I'll be back in a half hour," he said. "Nice wristbands, by the way."

I listened to him close and lock the front door.

I listened to him back down our driveway.

Our house was so quiet.

I took off the wristbands.

Even though I was still drained, I couldn't fall back asleep.

I decided to put on my headphones and listen to Will's mix.

The first song was, of course, "Fight Test." I remembered Will saying that it had something to do with how we met. So I decided to call him.

"Hallelujah, your phone's back on," he said. "I wanted to call, but my mom said I should let you rest." I let him ramble on about the yearbook and the letter he'd written me and some research he'd done on the Internet about amnesia and whatever else popped into his head.

"So, how'd I meet you anyway?" I asked him when he'd finally paused for a breath.

"I know this is gonna be hard to believe, but you didn't like me straightaway."

"No?" I said in mock incredulity.

"Indeed, my friend. I grew on you. I'm like that. I'm a grower. But officially, we met the first day of ninth grade in an informational meeting for *The Phoenix*, but you know we didn't meet that day, not really. We just saw each other and exchanged names and went on about our business. The first time I really met you was about a month later. They had taught us how to lay out pages on the computer, and I was watching you work over your shoulder, which is something you despise though I didn't know it at the time—"

I interrupted, "Actually, that's something everyone despises."

"Right, that's good advice there, Chief. I'll make a note. Back to how we met, you pasted a picture of the cheerleading team onto the page and it was starting to look really nice, but it made the copy shift so that only the first line of the caption paragraph was left on the bottom, what they call—"

"An orphan, I know." I didn't know how I knew, but I did.

"Hey, you remember! That's a good sign. I said to you, 'Sucks about the orphan.' And you turned around and gave me a look like you wanted to kill me. You thought I was talking about you being adopted—"

"You know about that?"

"I'm telling you I know everything about you," Will said. "Unfortunately, not at the time, though. So I repeated the thing about the orphan, and you said, 'Screw you,' and it might have gone on like that forever except that I finally said, 'I'm talking about the copy.' And then you laughed and said, 'Yeah, I think I'll make the picture a little smaller to get rid of it.' That's how we met. And about a month or so later, after we knew each other better, you mentioned you were adopted, which cleared everything up enormously."

"'Cause before you were just thinking I was a bitch?"

"I wouldn't say that."

"What does the song have to do with us meeting though?" I asked.

"Well . . ." Will cleared his throat. "I guess, on some level, it's about the difficulty of modern communication. Like I said, I didn't have that much time to put together a proper mix. But I always think of you and meeting you when I hear it. Don't you do that? Don't you hear a certain song and associate it with a person? They don't even have to know you're doing it."

"Sometimes maybe."

"And my dad really liked that song, too. He was a big fan of the Flaming—"

I yawned. I couldn't help myself. "I'm sorry. You were saying? Your dad . . ."

"Oh hey, you should get to sleep, Chief. You can call me again tomorrow, if you want, if you're feeling up to it."

"Hey, Will, can I ask you another question?"

"Anything."

"Would you say that I was really into Ace?"

"I truly doubt if I'm the best person to answer that."

"Who else, then?" I asked.

Will sighed. "Honestly, I would say that you were. Not that I've ever understood his appeal, but there you go."

"Why, though? Why him and not somebody else?" I really wanted to know.

I heard Will take a drink of water before he answered. "I'm not in your head, so I'm only theorizing here. I think you like being seen around with a good-looking jock. I hope that doesn't sound too mean."

"So you think I'm shallow?" I countered.

"I didn't say that. I think you're the swellest gal around, but I also think you're human. And you go to a school where it's not entirely a bad thing to have a boyfriend like Ace."

I wondered . . .

All this speculation was exhausting. "Night, Will," I said.

"Good night, Chief. Say, do you think you'll be able to come back to school with everyone else after Labor Day?"

"I don't know when I'll be back. I'm still pretty tired."

"Well, take it easy, okay? I'll pick up your schedule and all your assignments, so you don't have to worry about any of that."

"Thanks."

I got under the covers and listened to that song again. I fell asleep before it was over.

I slept for the next thirteen hours straight. I didn't even hear my dad come home.

The day before I was to return to school, I told Dad I wanted to figure out if I still knew how to drive.

"You sure you're ready?"

I wasn't necessarily, but it didn't seem particularly appealing to have my dad driving me everywhere either.

"It's only been about three weeks, kid. I'm just not sure it's safe."

But I had to start figuring these things out, you know?

We went out to the car. I put the key in the ignition and turned it. The movement seemed familiar enough.

I was about to step on the gas when Dad said, "You need to shift the car into reverse."

"Oh, right," I said as I did it.

I was about to step on the gas for the second time when Dad said, "You'll want to look in the rearview mirror to see who's coming. Then over your shoulder to check the blind spot."

"Right. Right." The road was empty in both directions.

I started to back up the car. I had just eased my bumper out of the driveway when a horn blasted three times. I slammed on the brakes as an SUV raced by, barely missing us.

Moron!" Dad yelled, though surely no one could hear him except me. "A lot of people speed through this area. Don't worry about it."

But I was worried about it. I didn't feel at all confident that I knew how to drive anymore. "I should *know* how to do this!" I banged my fist on the dashboard. Of all the things that had happened, this struck me as particularly humiliating. I felt childish and helpless and weak and stupid and suffocated. I hated that Dad or anyone else had to watch me be so pathetic. I needed to get the hell out of that car.

I didn't even turn off the ignition. I just slammed the door and ran straight to my room.

Dad followed me. "Naomi, wait! I want to talk for a second!"

I turned slowly. "What?"

"I'm . . . You'll drive when you're ready. We can try again next week. No rush."

Dad's eyes were bloodshot. He looked like he hadn't been sleeping, and he never slept much to begin with. "You look kind of tired, Dad."

Dad sighed. "I stayed up late watching a nature program. It was about lemmings. You know how people used to think they all committed suicide when the population got too big?"

"Sort of."

"Turns out they have really bad eyesight."

"Since when do you watch those?" I asked. My dad was not really a "nature" guy.

Dad shook his head. "Not sure. Since the divorce, I guess. I'll drive you to school tomorrow, okay?"

I hadn't been dreading school, but only because I hadn't been thinking about it.

In the hospital, they had tested my cognitive skills and concluded that my brain was, aside from the memory loss, normal. Whatever normal meant. (Or as Dad had joked, "No more weird than it was before.") I could remember math and science, but had forgotten entire books I had read and most of history, world and, of course, personal. I still had the ability to learn new things, and everything before seventh grade, so, all things considered, it could have been far worse. Some people with head traumas end up having months or even years of physical therapy where they have to be taught everything all over again—reading, writing, talking, walking, even bathing and going to the bathroom. Some people end up with their heads shaved or having to wear a helmet. I'm sure either would have gone over really well at my high school.

The main thing that worried me about school was not the work, but the kids. To look at me, no one would even think anything much had happened—all I had were bruises and some stitches—but inside, I felt different. I worried about not recognizing people and not acting the right way. I worried about having to explain things when I barely understood them myself. I worried about everyone staring at me and what they would say. This was why I'd tried not to think about school at all.

The next morning at Tom Purdue, most of the kids who were getting dropped off looked young, like freshmen or sophomores. Sitting in the passenger seat of Dad's car, I felt more than a little melancholy that I hadn't driven myself.

"You ready?" Dad asked.

"No," I replied.

I had written my schedule on my hand the previous night; I had a map of the school; I knew the combination to my locker; Dad had called all my teachers. Why was it so hard to open the car door?

Dad pulled a small, rectangular black box out of his jacket pocket. "Your mom wanted me to give this to you. It came last Friday."

"I don't want anything from her," I said.

"Fine by me. I'm just the messenger," Dad said.

Attached to the box was a gift card in her distinctive, artistic scrawl: "Cupcake, Dad said you could use these. Have a good first day back. I love you, Mom." But I wasn't her cupcake or anyone else's, and I hated being bribed. I didn't even care what was inside the box. I wouldn't like it on principle.

Then again, it's really difficult to resist opening a present once it's already right there on your lap.

So I lifted the lid. Inside was an extremely expensive-looking pair of silver-framed sunglasses.

I looked at Dad. "You told her about the light?"

"She's still your mother, kid."

A "fun" side effect of my accident was that I felt like I was living in the North Pole. Everything seemed incredibly bright (like I imagine the polar caps probably are in person) and I was usually freezing, even though it was still September. I guess this sort of thing can happen with head injuries. As it was explained to me, the wires in your brain have to reroute, and sometimes they send out incorrect or too much information. The upshot was that I was cold when it was warm and weirdly sensitive to light, even when it really wasn't all that bright.

Despite this, I was still going to toss Mom's present out the window onto the school driveway. I wanted someone to run over them with a car.

It was probably a reflex more than anything, but I made the mistake of putting them on.

The morning was bright—whether it was uncommonly so, I could not say for certain—and my head did throb less behind the lenses. When I looked in the passenger mirror, I saw that they also had the considerable merit of covering most of what was left of the bruising and even some of the scar that had formed over where my stitches had been.

I'll admit it. What truly sold me was completely shallow. I felt the tiniest bit cool.

Maybe it was because she was an artist, but my mom had good taste. I had to give her that. The woman always knew exactly what a person should wear.

"You look good, kid," Dad said.

I ripped the note in half, handing that and the box to him. "Would you mind throwing these out for me?"

I pushed the car door open and got out of Dad's car. I left the sunglasses on. Just because my mom was a gigantic slut was no reason to pass up a perfectly good pair of shades.

Four

PEOPLE WERE EITHER STARING AT ME OR AVOIDING my gaze entirely. I was glad for the sunglasses because no one knew which way I was looking. I thought I heard kids whispering my name, but I couldn't make out what they were saying. Maybe I didn't even want to know what they were saying. Maybe they weren't saying anything. Maybe it was all in my head.

I hadn't mentioned to Will or Ace that I was coming back to school that day. I hadn't wanted to make a big deal of it. Walking up the steps of Tom Purdue, I sort of wished I *had* told someone.

Once I was inside the main hallway, I scanned the crowd for a familiar face—James, Will, Ace—but I didn't see anyone I knew. Kids and even a few teachers said hello to me. I smiled in return. I had no idea who any of them were.

We had moved to Tarrytown the year I turned twelve. I had gone to Tarrytown Elementary for sixth grade before switching to Tom

Purdue for junior and senior high. Unfortunately, that's where my memory stopped. All these people were strangers to me. I felt like the new girl. Actually, it was worse than that. I'd been the new kid before, and at least then everyone knows where you stand. They *know* they don't know you.

I walked down the hallway to where my locker supposedly was, number 13002. I tried the combination that Will had given me in the packet with my schedule and assignments, but it didn't work. I tried it again. Still nothing. In frustration, I banged on the locker with my fist. Someone tapped me on the shoulder.

"You have to make an extra clockwise turn before stopping at the final number," said a very pale girl with dyed cranberry-red hair. She had on black worker boots with her kilt, and I could see rainbow-striped socks barely peeking out over the top of the boots.

I took her advice and the locker opened. "Thanks," I said.

"No problem, Nomi."

The girl looked familiar, though I couldn't quite place her at first.

"I know you," I said. She had been in my class at Tarrytown Elementary. Back then, Alice Leeds had had long blond hair that she often wore parted in braids. "Alice?" I asked.

"I didn't know if you'd remember me. Everyone's heard about your head."

I explained how I could remember everything before seventh grade, which included Mrs. Bloomfield's sixth-grade class.

"Are we still friends?" I asked her.

"Mmm, not so much. We sort of drifted, I guess." Alice shrugged. "See you around," she said as she left.

"See you."

I was wondering if we'd had a falling-out or if it was like she said, we'd just "drifted," when the bell rang. I tossed a bunch of books inside the locker and slammed it shut. I looked down at my hand where I had written "Precalculus, Mrs. Tarkington, 203."

When something happens, by which I mean something big like illness or death, there are some people who prefer to act as if nothing has happened. My homeroom and precalculus teacher, Mrs. Tarkington, was one of those people. While I didn't necessarily want anyone making a fuss, it was even more awkward when there was no mention at all.

Although all my teachers had been informed of my condition, Mrs. Tarkington did not waste time asking how I was or anything like that. She did not feel the need to tell me where my seat was either. A friendly boy with round glasses whispered to me, "Naomi Porter. We sit alphabetically. You're behind me. Patten, Roger."

"Thanks," I said.

I sat down, and he turned over his shoulder and shook my hand. "We're also on yearbook together. I'm not a creative like you; I just sell the ads in the back. Landsman got everyone up to speed on your condition. We were going to send a card, but luckily you got back pretty fast. Awesome glasses—"

"Mr. Patten, why do I hear whispering during the morning announcements?" Mrs. Tarkington asked.

"Sorry," I mouthed.

Roger smiled and shrugged.

As for the work, it was the beginning of the school year, so the class was still reviewing algebra II and trigonometry. Luckily, I remembered both.

Less luckily, I had somehow left my math book in my locker. Mrs. Tarkington lent me a spare, but you could tell it really put her out.

At the end of the class, Mrs. Tarkington pulled me aside. "Miss Porter, I let you get away with it today," she said, "but it is not acceptable to wear sunglasses in the classroom."

I tried to explain about the wires in my brain and all that, but you could tell she thought it was just an excuse. Maybe it partially was, but I still wanted to wear my sunglasses. I felt safer behind them. She waved her hand to dismiss me. "Don't do it again."

American history was second period, and none of it was particularly familiar. But then, it didn't seem like anyone else knew much more than me. Plus, it was all written down in the book, so I didn't think it would take much doing to catch up.

I got lost going to third period, English, because it was held in a room just off the school library that wasn't indicated on the map. When I finally got there, Mrs. Landsman embraced me as if I were her long-lost daughter. I took that to mean we were close.

"Naomi Porter, we were so worried about you!" Her hold was surprisingly tight for such a small woman, and Mrs. Landsman couldn't have been more than five feet one; I've been five feet seven since I was twelve, but with this little woman wrapped around my waist, I was suddenly very conscious of my height. She had Will's bright blue eyes, crooked smile, and pale skin. Unlike Will, her hair was reddish blond and it rained down to her waist: long, straight, and parted in the middle. She had the kind of gossamer doll face where you could tell it would be incredibly easy to hurt her feelings. The nameplate on her desk said her first name was Molly, and the name suited her: girlish, but old-fashioned; sweet and open like an apple.

"Will didn't mention you were coming back today!"

I confessed that I hadn't told him.

She wagged her finger at me. "My dear, he's going to be absolutely outraged!" All of Mrs. Landsman's sentences were whispery confessions ending in exclamation points. "He stayed home sick today—his stomach again—poor boy, he works too hard, but I have half a mind to call him right now!"

Mrs. Landsman embraced me again before directing me to a seat near the front of the classroom. "Please do let me know if I can help you with anything. Anything at all!"

Mrs. Landsman had begun the year with a drama unit, and the class was in the middle of reading *Waiting for Godot* aloud. All the parts had been divvied up during my absence, so I only had to listen to the other people read. The role of Estragon was read by a long-legged blond girl named Yvette Schumacher who was wearing maroon platform Mary Janes with kneesocks that had embroidered red hearts on them—in a school with uniforms, you spend a lot of time looking at the footwear for clues. I knew Yvette because she had also been in my sixth-grade class, along with Alice from the hallway. The role of Vladimir was played by Patten comma Roger from my precalc class.

Maybe if I had started the play from the beginning it would have been more interesting or made more sense. But without context or knowing the story, it was difficult even to know what the play was about. Were the main characters in love or just friends? It was hard to tell.

I tried to concentrate, but even when I was a little kid I hadn't particularly liked being read to. As soon as I learned how, I always preferred to do it myself. Plus, the language in the play was so circular that I found it extraordinarily difficult to follow out loud.

The next thing I knew, Mrs. Landsman was gently shaking me.

"Naomi, poor darling, wake up!"

The classroom was empty, and for a moment I forgot where I was. "I'm sorry."

"Don't apologize, dear. You can read the play later. It's fifty-something years old and will certainly keep until tomorrow. You looked so peaceful. I was considering letting you sleep even longer. Would you like to go to the infirmary for a quick rest?"

I really was exhausted, but I knew I'd better keep plowing through my schedule. It wasn't going to get any easier. "That's a really nice offer, but I should go," I said reluctantly.

"If you're sure . . ." Mrs. Landsman studied me with concern. "I think of you like one of my own, dear," she said. "I'll write you a note. What's your next class?"

I checked my hand. "Physics with Dr. Pillar."

"He's a lovely gentleman. One of my favorites!" As I was six inches taller than her, Mrs. Landsman had to reach up to put her arm around my shoulders. My dad and I weren't much in the way of huggers, but it felt nice to be touched by someone who wasn't either a doctor or trying to get in my pants. It felt nice to be mothered.

"You may want to stop in the washroom. A little bit of your schedule seems to have transferred to your face," she said.

In the girls' bathroom, I examined myself in the mirror. The backward stamp of my schedule was indeed on my right cheek. The soap was the rough, powdery kind you only ever find in schools. It was crap for cleaning. I had to basically rub my face raw to remove my schedule, and in the process of doing that, I smudged the part that was written on my hand.

When I finally got to physics the lights were off because the class was in the midst of watching a DVD: an introduction to subatomic particles and string theory. I handed Dr. Pillar my note, and he smiled and pointed me to a desk.

I took off my sunglasses and watched the movie. It was actually very relaxing. The narrator had one of those silky PBS type voices, and there was quite a bit of New Age and Philip Glass-y music to accompany the images, which were a combination of talking-head interviews featuring very nerdy adults in lab coats and short-sleeved polyester dress shirts, and computer simulations of stars and planets, forming and breaking apart and forming again. It was sort of beautiful. All those stars and planets, they reminded me of something . . .

Of being in an air-conditioned planetarium.

The air was stale like a library, but also sweaty like the sea . . .

Me in a flimsy white tank top.

With goose bumps on my arm.

Seventies rock.

A boy with sweaty hands.

This feeling . . .

Like anything might happen.

I wondered if this might be an actual memory, and if it was an actual memory, was it mine? Or was it something from a book I might have read or a movie I might have seen? Even when my brain had been perfectly functional, I had done that. Taken stories from books and sort of conflated them with actual events. Not lying exactly, though some might call it that. More like borrowing. It is hard to explain just what I mean unless you're the type of person who does it, too.

I turned my attention back to the program. One of the physicists in the program was saying something about how when scientists first started studying the universe, it was like being in a room in the dark. But now with the new theories, they realized it wasn't a room, but a house. Not any old house either, but a mansion with an infinite number of rooms to stumble through. I was imagining these scientists groping around in this darkened mansion. I don't know why but I pictured the scientists as a group of drunken women, like they'd just come from a frat party. "Oh hey," one would say to the other, "does anyone remember how in the hell we got in here in the first place?" They were still trying to get out when I fell asleep for the second time that morning.

Luckily, I woke up on my own this time, which was good. I didn't want to be known as "that chick who's always falling asleep in class." (There's always one; you know who you are.)

The doctors had said that head traumas can cause exhaustion for "a while."

"How long is *a while*?" I asked.

"Ballpark?"

"Ballpark."

They nodded and whispered to each other. "Indefinitely" was their very helpful reply.

"Miss Porter." Dr. Pillar stopped me on the way out. He had a perfectly round face and was bald with a woolly strip of jet black hair above his ears and neck, like a pair of headphones that had slipped off his head. "Your papa. He calls to say that your math and science skills are hunky-dory, yes?" He had a strange, stilted way of forming sentences and an equally strange accent that I couldn't quite place, but had a hint of Dracula in it.

"You are one year ahead in math and science, so this is very good, yes? But I prepare for you a dossier with chemistry and mathematics necessary for mastery of physics." He handed me a large heavy envelope, crammed with papers.

In other words, a review. I thanked him. It was nice to know that the school was not peopled entirely with Mrs. Tarkingtons.

"It is interesting, this. Why you have lost some things and not others . . ." He studied me, much like you would expect a lab technician to watch an ape. "Maybe it is because you place different things in different areas of brain? We know nothing about brain, yes?"

It had certainly seemed that this was the case.

"And four years, is it? This is very odd. Maybe it is puberty onset that alters the place in which you are storing long-term memories? So you have everything before puberty, but nothing after?"

I wasn't sure what he was trying to say, but I really did not want to discuss puberty with Dr. Pillar.

"Perhaps a traumatic event from your youth that you have been very much longing to repress?"

"Um . . . perhaps."

"Forgive me. I like to make theories for what cannot be readily explained. It is my nature. Do you have any theories about your memory loss, Miss Porter?"

"I lost a coin toss and I fell down the stairs. Bad luck and clumsiness?"

"Or, perhaps, randomness and gravity. In this respect, you are walking physics experiment, yes?"

That was certainly one way to put it.

Fifth period was lunch, and Ace was waiting for me outside physics to lead me to our place in the cafeteria.

"You didn't say you were coming today!" He hugged me and lifted my backpack from my shoulder.

"It's fine, Ace. I can carry it myself."

"I want to," he insisted.

We sat with a group of about twenty kids at a long benchlike table. It was a mix of boys and girls, and I recognized some of them from my classes and a few others from elementary school. Our table was, by far, the noisiest one in the place. You could tell that the kids I ate with considered themselves to be the celebrities of the school. It was like they were putting on a show of having lunch as opposed to actually eating it.

A curly-haired blonde named Brianna introduced herself and then said, "I just want you to know how *brave* I think you are. What happened to you is so, so tragic. Isn't she so brave?"

I didn't feel at all brave. Even though her words were ostensibly addressed to me, she seemed to be talking to Ace or the table at large or the whole school.

She took my hand in hers. "It's strange because you look like yourself, and yet you're *so* different, Naomi."

"Different how?" I asked.

Brianna didn't answer. She had finished talking to me and was on to the next person.

Four or five of the people sitting nearest to me also introduced themselves. Some of the girls spoke too loudly, as if I were deaf. Others wouldn't quite look me in the eye. And then everyone just resumed *The Lunch Show* and ignored me, which was fine. I figured out pretty early on that these were Ace's friends, not mine. I wondered where James Larkin sat—I hadn't seen him yet. Or Will.

"Does Will usually eat with us?" I asked Ace.

"Why would you want to know about that?"

His reaction surprised me. "Did I say something wrong?"

"No . . . I know Landsman's your friend, but I just don't get that little dude at all." Ace shook his head. "He eats in the yearbook office. You sometimes eat there, too."

In addition to being loud, the cafeteria was kept at near-arctic temperatures, as if the administration was afraid our food might start to spoil while we were in the process of eating it. I actually started to shiver. On the way in, I had noticed kids eating in the courtyard. I said to Ace, "It's such a nice day, maybe we could eat outside?"

Before Ace could say anything, Brianna answered, "Um, I guess we could, but we always eat in here." Then Brianna and a girl whose name I couldn't remember giggled, like I had suggested we eat on Mars.

"It's true," Ace said with a shrug.

So I shivered through another ten minutes of lunch before telling him that I needed to get something from my locker.

"Do you want me to come with you?" Ace asked.

I shook my head and told him I was fine.

But I didn't go to my locker. I was simply tired of being cold. I walked out into the courtyard, but fall was near and it felt even colder to me out there.

I wandered behind the school. On the boundary between the athletic fields and the rest of campus was a greenhouse.

I tried the door and found that it was unlocked. It seemed somewhat less cold in there so I sat on a cement bench, in front of what appeared to be a cruel experiment with sunflowers—seven of the plants were mostly dead, but one was thriving. I wondered what the live one was being fed, or if it had just been more of a survivor to begin with.

I was still contemplating that eighth sunflower when a familiar deep voice said, "You're shivering."

It was James. I decided not to turn around and look at him yet. I didn't want to reveal how pleased I was to see him again, especially considering that he hadn't visited me in the hospital or at home.

"Maybe a little," I replied casually. "Is it cold in here, by the way? I have trouble telling."

"Not to me," James said, emerging from behind an orange tree with an unlit cigarette hanging from his lips. He placed the cigarette in his back pants pocket. "But that doesn't mean it isn't cold to you." He took off his jacket, which was brown corduroy with a sheepskin collar, and handed it to me. "Here."

I put the jacket on. It smelled like cigarettes and paint. "You smoke?"

"Now and then. Mainly to keep myself out of worse trouble."

For additional warmth I slipped my hands into his jacket's pockets. I could feel keys, a bottle of pills, a lighter, a pen, a few slips of paper.

"Suppose I should have cleared out my pockets before lending my jacket to a girl," he said. "What's in there anyway?"

I gave him my report.

"Nothing too controversial, right?"

Depends on what the pills are for, I thought. "Depends on what the keys are to," I said.

He laughed at that. "My mom's house. My car, which is, at the moment, in the shop."

Distantly, I heard the bell ring.

"You're still shivering," James said. He loosened his tie and took off his dress shirt. He had a T-shirt underneath. "Put it on under the jacket. You'll be warmer."

"Won't you get in trouble?" The dress code at Tom Purdue was pretty strict.

He said he had another shirt in his locker. His arms were slim and muscular, but not like a guy who worked out. I noticed a two-inch horizontal scar across his right wrist. I wasn't sure, but it looked like the kind of mark you'd get from trying to off yourself. He saw me looking at it. He didn't cover it up, but he didn't choose to explain it either.

The bell rang again. "You're going to be late," he said.

I looked at my hand. Sixth period was French III in Room 1—, the number had gotten smudged during the course of my morning ablutions. I held out my hand for James to read. "You wouldn't happen to know where this is, would you?"

He held my hand like a book. After he'd read it, he closed his hand around my palm and offered to take me himself.

I liked the way his hand felt over mine. It might have been my imagination but I thought I could still feel the faintest of scabs on his palm from where I'd grabbed him so hard three weeks ago.

He dropped my hand almost as soon as he grabbed it. When he spoke, his voice was hard and businesslike. "Come on. We'll be late."

I had barely kept up with him as he led me through the halls, but then, at the French classroom door, he lingered. I thought he might say something to me. All he wanted was his jacket. "My jacket," he said, rather testily for a person who had been so quick to take it off in the first place. I removed the jacket and was about to take off his shirt, too, but he repeated the thing about having another. "You should really dress more warmly," he said before rushing off without a single glance over his shoulder. I stood there, cold again, and feeling bad that I hadn't had time to thank him for his help at the hospital.

I had forgotten nearly all of French, which actually made my French class unintentionally fascinating.

"*Bonjour, Nadine,*" said Mme Greenberg in New York–accented French.

One thing that had never been in question was my name. "Sorry," I said, "My name is—"

"*En français? Je m'appelle . . .*"

"*Je m'appelle* Naomi. Uh . . . *Non, Nadine. Nadine, non.*"

"*Ici, nous employons les noms français, Nadine.*"

"*Oui,*" I said. Fine, if she wanted to call me *Nadine*, whatever. It sounded like the name of a *comment dit-on?* French prostitute, but whatever. *En anglais,* I asked the boy sitting behind me what in the hell she was talking about. Apparently, we had all been assigned French names, which struck me as incredibly idiotic. If I ever went to Paris, people weren't going to all of a sudden start referring to me as Nadine.

Seventh period was gym, which I was, of course, excused from, and had been told to use for study hall until I could rejoin. I spent the period sleeping.

Last period was Advanced Photography Workshop. The teacher's name was Mr. Weir. He didn't look all that old to me (he might have still been in his twenties, though I've never been good at guessing ages), but he was completely bald. Whether it was elective baldness or compelled, I couldn't determine. He was wearing a T-shirt and a pin-striped blazer. When I came into the room, he introduced himself. "I'm your favorite teacher, Mr. Weir. Fierce shades." I liked him immediately. "You sit over there," he said helpfully, pointing me to a table in the back.

Advanced Photography Workshop was for kids who'd taken two years of other photography courses, which I had (although I couldn't remember them, of course). The main point of the class was to do one big independent project. It was basically supposed to be a series of pictures that told a story, preferably a personal one, and our whole grade was based eighty percent on the one assignment, and twenty percent on everything else, which, from what I could tell, mainly came down to class participation. It seemed like a breeze to me, the fat on the rest of my schedule, something I could put off while getting caught up with my more academic subjects.

On my way out of the classroom, Mr. Weir asked if we could talk. "I don't know if I should mention this to you, but you came to see me in the summer before your accident. You told me you wanted to drop this class."

"Why?"

"You said something about commitments to yearbook, but I'm not really sure. That may have been an excuse, so as not to hurt my feelings. Of course, you can still drop the class if you want, but I'd be happy to have you."

I asked him if he knew what I'd been planning to take instead, but he didn't. The one class I had actually liked (and that seemed like a small time commitment) I hadn't even wanted to take. Who could make sense of any of it?

At least the day was over. Each period had required me to be a slightly different person, and that was exhausting. I wondered if school had always felt this way and whether it was like this for everyone.

I decided to go to the bathroom. Not because I actually had to go, I just wanted to be alone.

I was sitting in the stall when I heard Brianna come in.

She was talking to someone.

She was talking to someone about me. "Oh, I know, it was so awkward at lunch," I heard her say. "I mean, she looks the same, but she's not all there. She used to be so . . ." She sighed. "But now . . ." her voice trailed off. "So tragic. So, so tragic. And you know who I feel really awful for? Ace."

She was an idiot, but I didn't necessarily want to confront her either. What would I say? Besides, she was probably right. I stayed in the stall until she had left.

To tell you the truth, I found the whole thing pretty depressing.

I was still sitting there when my cell phone rang. I hadn't even realized it was on. I looked at the display. It was Will.

"Don't tell me you're at school," he said.

"Unfortunately," I answered.

"Now I'm pissed. My mother called me, but I didn't believe her. Why didn't you mention you were coming today? I would have definitely gone to school."

"Your mom said you were sick."

"Nothing that major." He said he'd had an ulcer when he was younger and now he had "this stomach thing" that sometimes acted up, so he'd stayed home. "But I would have shown up for you, Chief. And I'm here now anyway."

"If you're not feeling well, shouldn't you still be at home?"

"I never miss yearbook," he said. "You don't either. Where are you? I'll come get you right now."

"Sure, Will. I'm in the ladies'. Come on in."

"Um . . . you're not serious?"

"No. I'm not."

Will laughed. "Right. How about I meet you at yearbook, then? It's the classroom next door to Weir's. By the way, you should call your dad to let him know you're with me."

"Hey, Will?" I asked.

"What?"

"How come I was going to drop photography?"

"Photography. Photography. Okay, I think you said it was because you thought that the big project was going to take up too much of your time. Also, you didn't think it was right for your grade to be based on a personal story. I think you thought it left too much to chance. And . . . that's it, I think."

I could tell he was leaving something out. My dad always says to listen for the pauses when you want to know if someone's hiding something. I asked Will if there was anything else.

"Well. I'm theorizing here. But the first two years of photography are more technical. Like which cameras to use and lighting and processing and Photoshop. But advanced is more creative, more like what your mom does, if you know what I mean. So maybe that was the problem?"

I didn't say anything, but it sounded like truth. "I'll see you upstairs," I said.

The staff cheered for me when I entered the room and everyone sang "For She's a Jolly Good Fellow" and shook my hand and patted me on the back, like I was some kind of hero. Someone held up a camera that turned out to be *the camera*, and said that I should have my picture taken with my old nemesis. They rounded up yet another camera, and I pretended to be having a fistfight with *the camera*, which made everyone laugh. I felt a little overwhelmed and maybe even touched, because it was clear how much these people really did like me, as opposed to the ones I had to eat with in the cafeteria.

All that was wonderful, until I started to realize what the actual business of yearbook entailed. It amounted to a succession of group photos, selling advertisements, and going to conferences about (you guessed it) yearbooks. All this required an endless series of meetings and debates. I wondered why in the world it could possibly take so much time, money, and effort to slap two hard covers around a stack of photographs.

The meeting lasted until around seven o'clock at night. There were photos to approve and copy to edit and schedules to arrange. On the way out, I asked Will how many times yearbook met each week. He laughed and said, "You're joking, right? We meet every day. Some weekends, too."

I did the math. That amounted to twenty (plus) hours a week of yearbook.

Seven hundred and twenty hours a school year—not including weekends or yearbook conferences.

Any way you looked at it: a *hell* of a lot of time.

I hoped that I would get my memory back, so that I would remember what I had liked about yearbook in the first place. I didn't want to let all these nice people down.

In the car on the way home, Will couldn't stop talking yearbook. The guy was obsessed, and I guess with seven hundred twenty hours a year, you'd have to be. I mainly found myself ignoring him. I'd nod every now and again and that seemed to be all the response that was required on my part.

I wanted to ask him why he (I) liked yearbook so much, but I thought it might hurt his feelings.

"You're awfully quiet," he said.

I told him I was tired, which I was.

"I've been talking too much," he said. "I guess I just got excited that you were back. It's not anywhere near as much fun without you, Chief."

We were halfway to my house and stopped at a red light when I spotted James Larkin walking along the sidewalk. It had started drizzling, and even with whatever strangeness had passed between us in the greenhouse, I felt like we should offer him a ride. I asked Will if he would mind pulling the car over, and he replied, "The chap looks like he wants to be by himself."

I reminded him how much James had helped me in the hospital, and how I had never had a chance to really thank him. "Plus," I added, "he was nice enough to return the yearbook camera." I knew that last part would definitely get Will. He sighed like it was really putting him out and muttered something about it "costing a lot of money to keep starting and stopping the car all over the place." So I told him he could just drop me off, that I'd walk the rest of the way home. "Yeah right, I'm really going to leave my injured friend in the rain," he said. "I don't have all day to chauffeur you and your buddies around."

I got out of the car and called James's name. "Do you need a ride?" He turned real slow, and for a second after he saw me I was pretty sure he was just going to keep right on walking. Finally, he ambled over to Will's car. He didn't look all that enthusiastic about seeing me again. I was starting to wonder if I had hallucinated the boy I had met in the hospital.

"Still cold?" he asked politely.

"A little," I replied. "Your shirt's in my locker."

James shrugged.

I was about to say how I'd been hoping we'd run into each other again when Will decided to get out of the car. Will edged himself between James and me and stuck out his hand. "Larkin, nice to see you, and thanks again for dropping off the camera. Naomi's the other editor of the yearbook, not that you asked."

"I did not know that," James said. His mouth threatened to smile for a second. "Well, it was . . . good seeing you both."

"The thing is," I said, "I was sort of hoping I'd run into you again. I didn't get a chance to thank you for all your help at the hospital—"

James cut me off. "Really. Don't mention it," he said. He stuck his hands in his coat pockets and turned to walk away.

"Wait!" I called out. "Can't we at least give you a ride?"

Will pinched me on the arm and muttered, "He doesn't want a ride."

But Will shouldn't have worried, because James just shook his head. "It's not raining that hard."

We got back in the car, and Will started chattering about yearbook again. "It would be really great, for once, to have some decent artists on staff."

"Is he an artist?"

"Who?"

"James."

"I think he does something with video, I'm not sure. The point is, all the good ones go over to newspaper or lit mag or even drama, but none of them ever want to work yearbook. And it's so stupid when you think about it. 'Cause no one's even gonna see the lit mag or the newspaper like a week after it comes out. But everyone's gonna have their yearbook when they're really old. You know? Hey, Chief?"

"What?" We were stopped again at that same light, and I was watching James cross the street.

"Forget it," Will said.

"What's his story?" I asked.

"How am I supposed to know?"

"Aren't you supposed to know everything? He was kind of rude, don't you think?"

Will shrugged. "No, he just didn't want a ride."

At that moment two things happened. The traffic light turned green, and it began to pour. "I suppose we should offer him a ride. Again." Will sounded about as unenthusiastic as it is possible for a person to sound. He drove up alongside James.

"James!" I leaned over Will and yelled through the driver-side window.

"I don't mind the rain!" he yelled. His hair was already soaked.

"James," I said, "get in the car, would you?"

We locked eyes for a second. I raised my eyebrow. He shook his head the tiniest bit.

"I'm fine," James repeated.

"But it's storming," I protested.

"Listen, Larkin, she's not gonna give up, and I'm wasting gas. Just get in already," Will barked.

James obeyed Will.

"Thanks," James said to Will.

"Where to, sir?" Will asked.

"Just my home, I guess," James said. He gave a few directions, and Will indicated that he knew where that was. In the rearview mirror, I watched James take off his jacket, which had gotten wet. I could see that leather cord with the ring on it again.

Will had noticed the ring, too, and he asked, "What's the ring?"

"Oh, it's my brother's," James said, slipping the ring under his T-shirt.

"Why isn't he wearing it then?" Will asked.

"I guess that'd be"—he paused to dry off his hair on his shirt— "'cause he's dead."

"Hey," Will said, "I'm really sorry about that, man."

James shrugged and said something about it having happened a long time ago. It was clear to me that he didn't want to talk about it, so I changed the subject. "I've been thinking. You never came to visit me in the hospital."

"Yeah . . . I meant to. But I don't really *love* hospitals."

"I was waiting," I said, turning around to look at him through the gap between the headrest and the front seat. "And you could have visited me at home, too." My sunglasses slipped down the bridge of my nose a bit, and James reached into the gap to push them back up. He let his finger lightly graze the space above my brow before returning his hand to his lap.

"Does it still hurt?" James asked.

"Not too much," I said.

"Do you remember what happened?" he asked.

"Nope, she doesn't know anything past sixth grade," Will answered for me, which was annoying. He was behaving rather badly.

I turned back around. "That's not entirely true. I do still remember math and science."

"What more is there in life?" Will quipped.

"I've just forgotten everything else," I continued. "I'm basically a blank slate."

James laughed. "Lucky girl."

"I don't see what's so lucky about it," Will grumbled.

"Aren't there things you'd rather forget?" James asked him.

"No," Will said. "There are not. If I were Naomi, I'd be screaming mad."

"Well, are you?" James asked me.

I thought about it for a second before shaking my head. "Not really. There's nothing I can do about it, is there?"

James nodded. "That's an awfully mature attitude. I still get plenty pissed about things I can't do anything about."

Like what? I wondered, but didn't say. "Besides, my memory might still come back."

James's house was on its own private road. The house was gray stone and not really a house at all. A mansion, I suppose. It would have seemed larger had it not been in the middle of an even more expansive lot. It reminded me of estates I'd seen in France when my parents had "wandered" there the summer I was seven. I didn't even know they had such houses in North Tarrytown.

James had no neighbors, and even though it was already evening, there wasn't a single light on that I could see. It seemed lonely. I wondered how many people lived there.

Despite Will's plaintive looks, I got out and walked James to his door. The knocker on the door was an enormous iron lion's head. Its nose and eye were badly dented. It reminded me of myself.

"I probably would have freaked out if you hadn't been there. I didn't get a chance to tell you before."

"I'm glad I could help," he said.

"I wanted to call you, but I didn't know your number or anything. So, well, thanks, I guess." I reached out to shake his hand.

"How formal," he said. He surrounded my palm with his other hand before gently squeezing it.

We seemed frozen in that handshake, and then Will honked the car horn.

"I think your friend wants to go," James said. He let my hand drop and said coldly, "I should go, too. Thank him for the ride."

I decided not to take James's sudden changes in temperature personally. Some people were like that. He'd been kind to me when I'd needed someone and to expect anything more would be unreason-

83

able. I'd thanked him now and that was enough. Besides, I already had a boyfriend.

As he was pulling out of James's driveway, Will asked me, "What the heck took so long?"

I said how I'd just been thanking James again, and Will said, "That kid's a strange duck."

I asked him what specifically he meant.

"Well, and I don't know if this is true, but when he transferred here, they said it was because he went crazy over some girl at his old school."

I asked him what specifically he meant by crazy.

"Like stalking her and making threats. That kind of crazy. I heard the girl had to get a restraining order or something," Will informed me.

James didn't seem the type to me. If anything, he was overly respectful. Plus, he had that trustworthy voice. "How do you know it's true?" From what I could tell, everyone at school just liked to talk crap about everyone else.

"Do you want to know what his nickname was at his old school?"

I rolled my eyes.

"Crazy James."

"What's that supposed to mean?" I asked him.

"Duh, it means he's"—he twirled his finger in a circle around his ear in the universal sign of psychotic—"crazy. *Loco.*"

"That's the stupidest thing I've ever heard. It's not even a real nickname. It's his name and an adjective." Will was being so childish.

Will shrugged, as if to say, *Don't blame me.*

"You made up the whole thing with the nickname, didn't you?"

"No, of course not!" Will sighed. "Maybe. But the point is, it could have been his nickname. It was for illustrative purposes. All the other stuff was totally, totally true, Chief."

We got to my house and Will patted me on the shoulder. "Don't worry if all the yearbook stuff seems overwhelming at first. I'll pick up the slack until you're feeling completely up to snuff, okay?"

Will was fond of old-lady phrases like *up to snuff*, which probably would have amused me if I hadn't been feeling pretty annoyed with him at this point. "Thanks. Say, Will, why do we like yearbook so much anyway?"

About a million colors passed over Will's face. He began by sighing and that turned into a laugh. His brow furrowed for a second, and then his blue eyes seemed to cloud, like he might cry. He didn't cry though.

"Is it a hard question?" I asked.

"No. It's probably ludicrous . . . I just hoped it might be something you would remember on your own. I know it might seem lame to some people, but we both really believe in what we're doing. I'd say you even more than me. To us, it's not just a book with a bunch of pictures. It's an icon, a symbol. It gives the younger kids an ideal to aspire to, and the older ones who've graduated something to hold on to when the world is hard. We both really believe that it can define the school and the way people see the school. A good high school yearbook can make a better school. And better kids. And a better planet. And a better universe. We write the story of the year. If you think about it, it's a huge responsibility."

"Good speech," I said sincerely.

"I've given better. We used to always talk about all the things we would do when we were finally running the show. How we'd really include everybody in the yearbook, and make it democratic and personal at the same time. How we'd make sure it wasn't just pictures of the popular people and the athletes and the kids who were friends with people on the staff. You're all three, by the way."

"I am?" I knew the athlete part to be right, but I hadn't felt at all popular in my one day at Tom Purdue.

"Sad, but true. The only thing we ever worried about was which one of us would be made editor, because there was just one editor. By the time it came to interview last year, we had come up with a plan to apply together, to be co-editors, even though it was entirely unprecedented and fairly controversial, us being juniors and all. That's how we became the first co-editors in the history of *The Phoenix*.

"And now we are running the show. Pretty cool, right?"

I nodded, but, truthfully, I had found Will's whole speech disheartening. I could see and hear his conviction and, in contrast, I felt none of that. Maybe I had in the past, but I didn't anymore.

When we reached my house, Will got out of the car and walked me to the door. Like his mother, he hugged me surprisingly hard, then he patted me on the back twice to indicate that the hug was over. "Okay, Chief." He did this comical salute with his hand before returning to his car.

I was about to unlock my front door when I realized I didn't have any idea where I'd put my keys. I rang the doorbell, and about five seconds later Dad answered.

"I lost my keys," I started to say at the same time Dad said, "You forgot your keys this morning."

Dad asked me how my first day back had been, but I wasn't in any mood to talk. I told him I had a headache and went to my room to lie down.

Dad must have let me sleep, because I didn't wake up until my phone rang around nine-thirty that night.

"I've been thinking about your question. And I thought of another reason I like yearbook so much," Will said.

"Okay."

"You know that we both joined the staff in ninth grade, right? But what I didn't mention to you was the year before ninth grade had been pretty rough for both of us. You had the thing with your mom. I had some . . . family stuff, too. Well, I think yearbook sort of saved me. It gave me something to do every day instead of just, well, fixating, I guess. And for me at least, yearbook is sort of inseparable from you. You really are my best friend in the whole world, Chief."

I could hear all sorts of things in his voice. Tenderness. Worry. Love even. How odd to be someone's best friend and not really know them at all. I couldn't come up with anything to say, so I waited for him to speak again.

"I've been feeling sort of bad about this evening. I think I might have been, for lack of a better term, an ass," Will said finally.

"You were, but I forgive you," I said just before hanging up.

It was late and I was starving. I hadn't eaten anything at lunch and I'd slept through dinner. I walked down the hall to Dad's office. If I haven't mentioned it before, Dad's sort of a gourmet. All the years he and Mom had been wandering, he'd also been collecting recipes for the books. The only thing my mom knew how to make was dessert.

His office door was closed. I was about to knock but I could hear he was on the phone with someone. I didn't want to interrupt him—

Dad hated that—so I loitered in the hallway outside his door and waited for him to be finished. I wasn't meaning to eavesdrop, at least not at first.

". . . looks normal, but I'm worried, babe," he said. Silence, and when I next heard him his voice was muffled. ". . . psychotherapy . . ."

I wondered who Dad was talking to about me. Mom, maybe? But he wouldn't be calling her "babe" . . .

". . . break it slowly. Everything in its time."

Break *what* slowly? Was I still the subject? I tried to listen more closely, but he moved somewhere else in the room where I couldn't hear him at all. The next time I heard him he was laughing. It was definitely not my mother. "Caracas!" he said. "I wish I could . . ."

Dad had always traveled a lot for his job; in addition to the books he wrote with Mom, he wrote articles for travel and men's magazines. I concluded he was probably talking business. It made me resentful, actually. I hated being small talk, just another one of his stupid anecdotes. To tell you the truth, I didn't care who he was talking to. I didn't want to be anyone's topic of discussion.

As I stalked back to my bedroom, I vowed to be less anecdote-worthy. That way, people wouldn't talk about me over late-night phone calls or in the goddamn bathroom at school.

As much as it was in my control, I would be normal.

By the end of the week, I had obtained a doctor's note permitting the sunglasses, and I gleefully presented it to Mrs. Tarkington. "Well, it's certainly not orthodox," she said, but she wasn't the type to argue with something on hospital letterhead.

Other than that, I occasionally got lost; I occasionally heard people talking about me; I occasionally told them to go screw themselves. Under my breath, of course—I was *normal*. In order to tolerate our arctic cafeteria, I brought a couple of extra sweaters. I let Ace hold my hand in the hallways. I never went back to the greenhouse.

On Saturday night, my campaign for normalcy continued when I went with Ace to a party that a tennis buddy from another school was hosting. Ace didn't bother to introduce me to the friend—maybe I already knew him?—and I never figured out who he was on my own either.

For all practical purposes, Ace abandoned me nearly as soon as we arrived. He became enmeshed in an elaborate drinking game that involved shots, dice, quarters, darts, a bull's-eye, and chest bumping. Although I watched the game for about fifteen minutes, I came out with no sense of the rules or how the winner was determined. I suppose it was like any drinking game. Last man standing.

I'm not being fair. Ace did ask me a couple of times if I was having a good time. I lied and told him I was. To tell you the truth, I was glad that he was occupied because, aside from tennis, I hadn't been able to figure out one thing that we had in common. If our conversations were a play, they would have been like a high school version of *Waiting for Godot*:

> Ace: Do you remember that time Paul Idomeneo got really
> stoned and jumped off the roof onto his dad's trampoline?
> Me: No.
> Ace: Well, it was pretty awesome.
> Me: Sounds amazing.
> Ace: Yeah, that kid was hard-core as hell. So, do you remember
> that time . . .
> *(And repeat. Endlessly, endlessly repeat.)*

I suppose he was trying to be helpful, telling me little things that might jog my memory. Unfortunately, Ace had no sense of what would interest me, and I was too embarrassed/polite/normal to question him about anything important, like, for example, *What do I see in you?* From the stories he told, our relationship had consisted largely of a bunch of parties where people acted like jerks interspersed with the occasional game of tennis.

I probably should have broken up with him. I didn't, though, mainly for two reasons: one, I didn't want to end it if it turned out that I really did love him (and I still held out some hope that my feelings would all eventually come back to me); and second, I'm a little ashamed to say, though it was probably the more important one, being with Ace made school easier. He protected me from those nasty lunch girls. Despite my memory being gone, I wasn't a moron. With my multiple sweaters and not knowing who anyone was, I knew how I looked to people, and I knew how vulnerable my situation at school was without Ace to define me socially. Being with him went a long way in my campaign for normalcy.

Ace brought me a beer, which he opened for me. "I had to go to the fridge to get this. The ones in the coolers were all hot. Having a nice time?"

I smiled and nodded and watched him walk away.

But I wasn't having a nice time, and looking around the place, I wondered if anyone there was. Because everyone looked a little miserable just below the surface, even Ace with his inexplicable game.

I'm pretty sure the doctors had mentioned something about avoiding alcohol and it turned out to be very good advice. Another one of the "fun" side effects of my injury was that I couldn't hold liquor at all. Halfway through my first beer, I was starting to feel ever so slightly smashed. I decided to go look for a place to lie down. I made my way to a bedroom on the second floor, but it was occupied by other partygoers.

I wanted Ace to drive me home, but I couldn't find him anywhere. It was probably just as well. The last I'd seen him, he'd been pretty wasted and not in the greatest vehicle-operating condition.

I made my way out to the front lawn. I really wanted to get home. Unfortunately, the party was about twenty miles from Dad's house, so I couldn't walk. As I stood there puzzling it out, I started to have that déjà vu feeling. Had I been to this house before? Had I been in this situation? Might my memory be coming back? It wasn't any of those things, of course. The only reason it felt like déjà vu was because it was the most clichéd situation in the world—I was the star of a driver's ed video on designated drivers.

I called Will on my cell phone to see if he would pick me up, but he wasn't answering. I left him an incoherent, rambling, probably embarrassing message. I was too drunk to worry that my English teacher might be the recipient.

Reluctantly I called Dad at home, though I knew he wasn't likely to be there. He'd gone out with Cheryl and Morty Byrnes, travel writers who used to be Dad's and Mom's friends, but now were just Dad's. I had commented that it was strange, because Cheryl Byrnes had really been Mom's friend in the first place. Dad's response was that "In situations of infidelity, the cheated-on always gets all the mutual friends."

Dad didn't pick up the home phone so I dialed his cell. I cleared my throat and tried to make myself sound less drunk.

"Naomi," Dad answered, worried.

"Daddy," I said, and then I completely ruined my plan to sound less intoxicated by starting to cry.

"How much did you drink?"

"Just the one, I swear. I thought one would be okay."

I managed to explain to Dad where I was and he said he'd come and get me.

While I was waiting for Dad to pick me up, Will called me back.

Will also offered to drive me home, but I told him it was too late, I'd already called Dad.

"Where was Ace in all of this?" Will asked icily.

"The game," I answered.

"What game?"

"The rules to the game were unclear."

"Chief?"

"Oh, Will," I said. "Silly, silly Will. I have to wait for my daddy now."

"Honestly, Naomi. You aren't supposed to drink after a head trau—"

I hung up on him. The phone rang again, but I ignored it. I couldn't talk to anyone. I lay down on the sidewalk and concentrated on not throwing up. I set my purse on top of my stomach, like a flag so that Dad could locate me, or a grave marker, if he didn't.

I must have passed out because the next thing I knew Dad was helping me into the backseat of his car.

While I waited for him to get back in, I noticed that the car smelled like flowers. I was wondering what the scent was when I became aware that a red rose was floating just below the passenger-seat headrest. I wondered if I was having a vision. After some woozy contemplation, I figured out that the rose was attached to a dark-haired woman's bun.

"You're not Cheryl and Morty," I said, pointing my finger at her.

The woman shook her head. "No. I am not Cheryl-Ann Morty." She had a Spanish accent of some kind, and she sounded amused. "Who is this Cheryl-Ann Morty?"

"Do I know you?" I asked her, but by then my dad was in the car.

"Naomi, this is my friend, Rosa Rivera," he said.

"You were supposed to be out with Cheryl and Morty," I said, wagging my finger at him. "Why aren't you out with Cheryl and Morty?"

"Yeah, and you're not supposed to drink until you're twenty-one," Dad replied. "And especially not in your condition."

"One beer! Barely one. Oh, that's . . ." But I didn't complete the thought, because I passed out in Dad's car.

I don't remember when we dropped Rosa Rivera off or how I got into the house. I do remember throwing up on Dad's beige floors.

"I'm never drinking again," I said to Dad as he held my hair back while I threw up in the bathroom.

"Well, I'd say that's probably wise. At least for the time being."

"Who was that woman?"

"Like I said, her name is Rosa Rivera. She's a tango dancer."

I didn't find any of that particularly illuminating, but I was too screwed up to make him elaborate.

"She smelled like roses," I said about ten minutes later when we were back in the kitchen, where Dad was making me take two aspirins. "I don't have any friends who smell like roses. I don't have any friends at all."

"That's not true, kid."

The home phone rang. Dad answered it. Still standing, I set my pounding head on the kitchen counter. The porcelain tiles felt refreshing.

"That was Ace. He was really worried about you. He said you disappeared," Dad reported.

"True," I said. "True, true."

"I read him the riot act anyway."

"Daddy, I need to go to bed now."

My cell phone rang. It was Will. I handed it to Dad. "Tell him I'm okay, wouldja?"

"Hello, Will . . . Yes, Naomi's fine. Except for being grounded for the next week, she's fine."

"I'm punished?" I asked after he'd hung up.

"Well, mainly you're punishing yourself, but I thought I ought to add a little something. So you've got to stay in for the next week. Seems parental, don't you think?"

My head was pounding. "Could you start by sending me to my room?"

"Good idea, kid. Let's go."

Around three a.m., there were three rapid taps on my window. It was Ace. He asked me if it was okay if he came in; I flipped on the light, wincing at the brightness, and got out of bed to unlock the window.

This time when he vaulted himself over my shelf, he knocked

my dictionary off. It hit the floor with a booming thwack. "Oops," he said.

I hoped the noise hadn't woken Dad.

"Where'd you go?" he asked. "I was worried."

"Where'd *you* go?" I asked.

"We were just out back in the pool. All you had to do was look."

"You abandoned me." I had a headache and I was in no mood to be questioned by Ace. "I was totally alone. Did I seem like I was having a good time to you?"

"But, Naomi!" Ace protested. "You said that you were."

I had said that. It was true. I had observed Ace to be a very literal person, so arguing with him was probably pointless. Instead, I told him that I didn't feel well, which was also true.

"Go back to bed," Ace whispered. "I don't want to disturb you."

I did, and I thought Ace might leave, but instead he sat in my desk chair. "Can we, maybe talk? Just for a little bit?" he asked.

I wasn't really up for more conversation with Ace, but I guess I felt sorry for the guy. I turned onto my side and asked him what he wanted to talk about.

"Do you remember that time we were at my cousin Jim Tuttle's house in Scarsdale?"

"No," I replied. I stifled a yawn and prepared myself for another one of Ace's fascinating drinking stories.

"We were coming back from sectionals. You still had on your tennis whites. Your hair was in a ponytail. I love your hair that way. You reached up and took my face in your hands and you kissed me. I was totally blown away. We weren't going out then. I didn't even know you liked me. You were the first brainy girl who'd ever shown any interest."

"Brainy girl?"

"One who reads and stuff, not just for school. I liked that about you. We never had classes together or anything. But I'd seen you around, and I always thought a smarty like you'd go for a guy like Landsman." Ace paused to look at me.

"He's just my friend."

"When you kissed me that first time, you were still wearing your tennis wristbands. I took them off of you and set them on Jim's couch. We forgot all about them. That's why I got you another pair. I, uh, realized my gift must have looked pretty lame to you if you didn't know the context."

I nodded. Something about his story had put a lump in my throat. It might have been the way he told it more than the story itself, or I might have been weakened by my emerging hangover. In any case, I was somehow granted a solitary moment of X-ray vision and what I saw was this: Ace was probably as frustrated with me as I was with him, and the only thing stopping him from breaking up with me was that he was, when it came down to it, pretty decent.

He knelt down beside my bed. His breath was bittersweet with alcohol. For a second, I worried I might throw up again, but the feeling subsided.

I took his face in my hands, the way he had described, and I kissed him.

Ace started stroking my hair (which was pleasant, but not romantic—it made me feel like a well-behaved lapdog), and he whispered so low I could barely hear him. "I don't want to pressure you. I don't want to be, you know, that guy who pressures you. Do you think we might have sex again someday?"

Without even thinking about it, I sat up in bed and pushed his hand away. "No."

He replied, "I didn't mean tonight necessarily."

I hadn't meant just tonight either, but I didn't say that. I told him that I'd gone off the pill, which I had.

Ace smiled all dopey and drunk. "Maybe we could do it at homecoming?"

"Homecoming?" I asked.

"Yeah. It's in three weeks. We're still going, right?" Ace explained that we had planned to before my accident.

I said yes. I mean, why not? I didn't remember ever having been to a homecoming dance.

Ace fell asleep on my bedroom floor. I couldn't, so I just lay in bed staring at him. He reminded me of a six-foot-four baby—he had long downy eyelashes and was drooling. It was more than just physically, though. Sleeping on my floor, he seemed somehow undefined and vulnerable. I even felt a certain tenderness for him. I wondered if that was the same as love.

When I awoke the next morning, Ace was gone. Actually, I should say afternoon. Dad had let me sleep in until around two before knocking on my door. "I'm making eggs."

I informed him that I couldn't eat anything, but Dad insisted it would make me feel better.

"Last night, I don't know if you remember, my little lush, but I was kind of out with someone . . ." Dad blurted out in the middle of pouring me orange juice.

"The woman with the flower in her hair?" I asked.

Dad nodded. "It was a date."

"Yeah. I figured that out on my own," I said.

"Smart girl." Dad started fussing with the eggs. They had started out as a goat cheese omelet but had ended up scrambled.

"If you play with them too much, they won't turn out," I pointed out to him.

"It's good advice. I'm the one who always says that." Dad beat the half-cooked eggs furiously. "Maybe I ought to start over?"

"Taste the same either way," I said. "This woman . . . is she someone Cheryl and Morty set you up with?"

"No," Dad said.

"Were you even out with Cheryl and Morty last night?"

"Not exactly."

I raised my eyebrow at him. "Jesus, Dad, were you lying to me?"

I thought about Dad saying he was getting coffee and his strange, secret phone calls. In other words, it wasn't his first date with the flower woman. He obviously had been seeing her since before my accident. "You've been hiding this from me since I got out of the hospital, haven't you? Why would you do that?"

"It looks bad. I know how it looks, but in my defense, I wanted to break things to you slowly. You had so much to take in with your mom, the divorce, having a sister and everything. I didn't want to add to your load."

"But you lied to me! What makes you think I'd even care if you had a girlfriend?"

"She's not just my girlfriend."

"What do you mean?"

For the longest time, Dad wouldn't answer me or look at me. The only sound in the kitchen was the hissing eggs, which were getting good and burned. I hadn't had much of an appetite for them to begin with.

"I'm getting married, kid," Dad said. He looked up at me guiltily.

Dad was getting married.

"She's a dancer. How 'bout that?"

Aside from the flower, I hadn't gotten much of a look at her in the car. In my head, I pictured the exotic kind. You know, a stripper, probably my age, with DDD breast implants and a fake tan, so I insisted he clarify. "What *kind* of dancer?"

When he said tango, I was slightly relieved. "She's traveled the world. She's won just about every award a professional tango dancer can win." He sounded the way he did when I'd brought home a particularly good report card. Proud, I guess. "Now she mainly teaches here and in the city."

He told me they'd met a year ago. He'd had to take dance lessons for an article he had been writing for a men's magazine. When everyone partnered up, he'd been the odd man out. "She had to take pity on your old man," he said.

"Do I like her?" I asked.

Dad cleared his throat. "It's been difficult for you. With Mom. And everything."

That meant I didn't like her.

"But maybe your injury could be an inadvertently fortuitous event?" Dad said. "A good thing. A new start."

A new start? That kind of talk didn't sound like my dad at all. There was nothing good about what had happened to me. Except maybe meeting James, and that had turned out to be a pleasant but anomalous event that had momentarily distracted me from how much everything else sucked.

"There's nothing good about this," I yelled. I grabbed Dad's keys off the kitchen island and ran out the door and straight into his car, which was parked in the driveway. I didn't necessarily plan to try driving again; I just wanted to be alone. I couldn't be in the same physical space with Dad.

Sitting in the driveway, I really wished I could go somewhere. Anywhere.

Dad came out about a minute later. He must have tended to the incinerated eggs first. I pressed the button that locked all the doors, so he couldn't get in the car.

"Naomi." His voice was muted through the window. "Please let me in."

I put my brain-damaged head on the steering wheel. It made the horn beep, but I didn't mind. I just let it blare. The horn was screaming for me and saying all the curse words that were running through my head. It was so satisfying that I sat like that for a few minutes. I would have let it go on even longer except my head started to throb from the racket.

"Naomi," Dad said after the noise had stopped.

"I don't want to talk about it," I yelled.

"This has gone badly. It was a stupid way for me to tell you about my getting married," Dad's voice was still tinny and distant through the glass. "And that crap I said about your head injury being a good thing. Of course I don't think that."

"Just go away!"

"Please let me in, kid. I feel like an asshole standing out here like this. At least roll down the window a little."

Dad was trying. He always tried.

Every year for my birthday, my dad gave me a single book. He always put a lot of thought into the selection. It was a big deal to him, because books in general are a very big deal to him. When Dad says he's going to church, he actually means that he's going to a library or a bookstore. For my third birthday, he gave me *Harold and the Purple Crayon*; for my tenth, *Holes*; for my twelfth, the last birthday I could remember, *A Tree Grows in Brooklyn*. He would inscribe the books, too. The messages were long and detailed, sometimes sentimental and usually funny. This was how he talked to me. This was how he told me the important things.

I didn't unlock the door, but I pressed the button that lowered the window.

"What book did you get me for my sixteenth birthday?" I asked.

"Why are you thinking about that?"

"I don't know. I just am."

"*Possession* by A. S. Byatt."

I couldn't remember having read it, which of course didn't mean that I hadn't. I asked him why he had chosen that one.

"It's about a lot of things, but mainly it's a love story. I was worried that you had gotten a bit, well, cynical with everything that had happened between your mother and me. I wanted to remind you about romance. It was probably a stupid notion. A sixteen-year-old who's not an expert on romance ought to be brought to a lab and dissected." Dad laughed. "I was considering *Jane Eyre*, but I know how you feel about orphan stories."

"What's her name again?" I asked finally. Something to do with flowers, or had she just smelled like them?

"Rosa Rivera," he said.

"Do I call her Rosa?" I asked.

"No, you call her Rosa Rivera. Everyone does."

"Why?"

"I always assumed it was because of the enticing alliteration of her first and last names." I couldn't tell if he was serious.

"What do you call her?"

"My darling, mostly," he said with tender notes I'd never heard him use before. "Sometimes my love."

I studied my dad. He was like an alien version of himself. I wondered how long he'd been this way.

When I was back inside, I called Will. He was my only source of reliable information, though I was starting to question how reliable anyone was. Ask two people to tell you anything, you'll get two versions. Even easy things like directions, let alone important or semi-controversial topics like why a fight started or what a person was generally like. If you don't know something for yourself, you just can't be sure.

"Did you know my dad was getting married?"

"Of course. In June," Will answered. "And nice talking to you, too."

"Why didn't you tell me?" I demanded.

"Well, it's not exactly your favorite subject. And I assumed your dad would have covered that."

"Why don't I like her?" I asked him.

"Basically, you think she's fake and trying to be your mother,"

Will said. "Something along those lines. And you said she smelled funny, like an old lady. One time, she bought your dad a gray fedora for his birthday. You thought it made him look, uh, effeminate, and then you donated it to Goodwill without telling him. To this day, I don't think he knows what happened to it."

"I gave away my dad's hat?" What a weird thing for me to do.

"Well, you really were not fond of that fedora," Will answered. "Your dad *would* probably look better in a bowler."

"Do you like her?" I asked him.

"I've only met her once, but she seemed all right. She's not gonna be my stepmother, though."

"But my dad . . ." It was hard to talk about Dad this way. "He really *loves* her, doesn't he?"

"Yes, Chief, I suspect he does."

On Wednesday, Dad suggested we go to Rosa Rivera's house in Pleasantville for dinner. Since our meeting (reunion?) seemed unavoidable, I agreed. Besides, I was grounded anyway.

When she answered the door, the first thing I noticed was that she definitely looked older than Dad. She had her black hair in a tight bun and was wearing her work clothes, which consisted of black tights, a black leotard, a black shawl tied around her waist, and high heeled shoes. Pretty much everything she wore was black except for her lipstick and the rose tucked behind her ear, which were both a dramatic crimson. Dancing had given her really excellent posture. I stood up straighter just looking at her.

She greeted me before she even greeted Dad. "Naomi," she said, throwing her arms around me and kissing me on both cheeks. "How are you, my baby?" She didn't have much of an accent, but all her *y*'s came out sounding like *j*'s—*How are joo?*

I thought about the question. "Cold," I said finally.

"Come inside, and I will try to warm you up."

Her place was the opposite of Dad's house. It was bursting with color, almost as if she had been given a mandate to use every crayon in the Crayola box at least once: turquoise walls, a fuchsia velvet sofa, a golden chandelier with midnight blue crystals, black-and-white-checkered marble floors, and red roses everywhere.

"Will you live here?" I asked Dad.

"It hasn't all been settled yet, but I think she'll probably move in with us."

I wondered what Dad's beige house would look like after they were married.

While Rosa was in the kitchen getting me a cup of tea, I examined the many framed photographs that were scattered about the room. One was of my dad and her. A few were of Rosa Rivera at dancing competitions. She also had three or so pictures of herself pregnant, presumably with the subjects of the bulk of the photos: two girls at many different ages doing the usual sorts of childhood activities.

"Those are her twin daughters, Frida and Georgia," Dad said. "They're both in college now."

"How old is Rosa Rivera anyway?" I whispered to Dad.

"Forty-six," Rosa Rivera answered as she came into the room with a teapot on a tray. "Your father is my younger man. He is six years my junior." *Yunior.* "My first husband was thirty years older than me, so it all works itself out, yes?" *Jes.*

She set the tray on an enormous lime-green hassock and joined me at the fireplace, where she put her arm around my shoulders. It was just the way she was—always kissing and touching you. My instinct was to move away, but for some reason I didn't.

With her other hand, she pointed to one of the dance competition photos. "This was my husband. He was also my dance partner for fifteen years."

"What happened to him?"

"He died," she said, blowing a kiss to the photograph.

"You really like pictures of yourself pregnant," I commented.

"It is true. Some people do not like it, but I loved being pregnant. I would not have minded being pregnant even more than I was, but my job made this difficult." *Yob.*

I thought of my mother and how she had never been pregnant with me.

"You are shivering," Rosa Rivera said to me. She put her hands around mine. "They are like ice!" she said, more to Dad than me.

"She's been that way since she got out of the hospital," Dad told her.

Rosa Rivera left the room and came back with a rainbow-striped silk scarf. It must have been twelve feet long. She was able to drape it loosely around my neck five times. It smelled like her.

"Better?" she asked.

"Warmer, at least."

"It suits you," she said.

I didn't think so, but whatever.

"You will take it when you leave."

"I couldn't," I said. It must have been really expensive. I didn't want her damn scarf anyway.

Rosa Rivera shrugged her super-straight shoulders. "I give everything away. I believe, Naomi, that your possessions possess you, do you know?"

I wasn't sure.

Dad went into the kitchen to make the salad, leaving Rosa Rivera and me alone.

I looked at her and wondered what I hadn't liked about her before. I decided to ask. "My dad says we don't get along," I said.

Rosa Rivera smiled at me conspiratorially. "Possibly. But I am an optimist, and I always believed you would come round."

She was wrong. I hadn't yet, and I didn't like her telling me that I had. I didn't want optimism; I wanted honesty. I unlooped the scarf from around my neck.

"Naomi," Rosa said, "I know this all must be very frightening for you." She put her hand on my arm, but I shook her off.

"What the hell would you know about it?" I asked.

I didn't wait for her reply. I just left her standing in her Technicolor living room, still reaching out her hands to me.

In the car on the way back, Dad was unusually quiet, and I suspected that Rosa had probably told him about my walking out on her before dinner.

He didn't say anything until we were back on our street. "Why didn't you let Rosa Rivera give you that scarf?" he asked.

I told him how it wasn't my style.

"Thought it looked nice on you, kid."

"Honestly, Dad," I said, "it's hard enough figuring out anything about myself without other people dictating my taste to me."

"I'm sure it is. But in any case, that wasn't what I was saying. I think I was talking courtesy, if you know what I mean?" All this was said casually.

He turned into our driveway. "Because sometimes, when someone wants to give you a gift, the best thing to do is accept it. Just an infinitesimal something I've learned that I thought I'd pass on to you."

I remembered how Dad, when he was still married to Mom, was always returning the presents she'd get him. Even if it was small, like a sweater. I used to think, just keep the stupid sweater, Dad. She obviously wanted you to have it. But my dad had been raised without much money, so he could be kind of strange around presents. Obviously, Mom knew his history, but even as a little kid, I could tell all his returning hurt her feelings.

I wondered if Rosa had felt that way when I tore that scarf off.

The worst of it was, what did I really know about my taste anyway? It had been a nice scarf and I had been cold, and if I was honest, maybe I had only been using that taste excuse as a way to hurt her feelings.

"Rosa wanted me to apologize to you," Dad said before we got out of the car.

"For what?"

"Something about your amnesia. Something about her saying she knew how you felt."

I nodded.

"But Sonny, her husband who died? He had Alzheimer's disease. Do you know what that is?"

I nodded again.

"So Rosa Rivera has had some experiences with memory loss. I think that's all she was trying to say. It probably came out wrong. It's sometimes hard to talk to— It's sometimes hard to talk. She didn't ask me to tell you any of this. I just thought you should know."

For a second, I felt like a jerk. Then I exploded at Dad. "I don't see what any of that has to do with me! Not to mention, you lied to me. Not to mention I obviously didn't like Rosa Rivera before, so why are you expecting me to like her any better now?"

"Well, Naomi, you were being ignorant then, so I had rather hoped you'd prefer to be enlightened now."

"I'll stick with ignorant, thanks." I tried to say this as dryly as possible.

Dad turned off the ignition, but he didn't move to get out of the car.

"I banged my head. That doesn't make me a different person. And it doesn't mean I'm going to like your goddamn fiancée either."

Dad shook his head and he looked as sad as I'd ever seen him. "You're just like me, kid, and it worries the crap out of me right now. Because with the current state of things, it's not necessarily a good thing to be like us. You're going to need to let people in."

I didn't say anything.

Dad got out of the car. "Don't forget to lock the door when you come in."

That night in my bedroom, I took out my sophomore yearbook for the first time since I'd been back to school. I had originally been intending to look through it for inspiration for my photography project proposal, which was due the next day. Instead, I found myself turning to my class picture.

There she was with her light gray hair and her dark gray lips upturned into an impenetrable grin. I wished that she could talk and tell me everything she had ever felt or thought or seen.

"What were you like?" I asked her. "Were you happy? Or were you smiling because they told you to?"

I looked at myself in my closet mirror and tried to arrange my features like the girl in the yearbook. I didn't quite have the trick of it yet.

I brushed some strands of hair in front of my face, the way the girl in the yearbook had worn hers. It looked wrong, though I couldn't say exactly why at first. I studied myself some more before deciding that the pieces of hair in the front had gotten too long.

I took a pair of scissors from my desk drawer and cut a few pieces on each side of my head. The easy swish of the blades against my hair was satisfying.

I looked in the mirror to check my work. I hadn't cut it evenly, so I took a little more off on each side.

Then, a little more.

As I cut, it occurred to me that it might be pointless to even try to look like the girl in the yearbook. It might be easier to be somebody completely different instead.

I cut pieces from the back and the front, until all that survived was a choppy short mane. With each piece, I felt like I was getting rid of someone's expectations of me: goodbye, Mom, Dad, Will, Ace, those kids at lunch, my teachers, everyone. I felt giddy and light, like I might even start to float away. It was the end of normal.

The girl in the yearbook would never have had short hair.

I set the scissors on my desk, gathered up the strewn clippings as best I could, and then I fell quickly, peacefully asleep. I didn't even take off my clothes or turn off the light.

When my alarm went off the next morning, I jumped out of bed without even looking in the mirror. I had actually forgotten all about my hair until I was in the shower. Little pieces slipped through my fingers like sand before they washed down the drain.

When I saw myself in the bathroom mirror, I felt sort of elated. It seems strange to say even now, but I finally recognized the person in the mirror as the person inside my head.

"Your hair!" Dad said when I came into the kitchen for breakfast. "What happened?"

I told him that nothing had happened. I had simply decided to cut it. I didn't ask him what he thought either.

"If I'd known you wanted to cut it, I could have taken you somewhere to get it done."

When I sat down at the table, Dad stood so that he could better appraise my mane from an overhead angle.

"It's not bad. It's cool actually. Kind of punk rock," Dad said finally, gently tousling my hair. "I barely recognize you, kiddo."

That hadn't been the point, of course. Maybe just an amazing perk. If no one recognized me, they wouldn't be upset when I didn't recognize them either.

I am

Five

Ace walked right past me in the hallway. I had to call his name, and when he saw me he looked confused and betrayed, like Bambi when his mother bites it in the movie. "I liked it long," he said finally. Then he kissed me. "It's going to take some getting used to." When we stopped kissing, I noticed that Will was staring at us from across the corridor.

I waved at him.

"Jesus, I thought Zuckerman was cheating on you, Chief," Will called.

"He'd love that," Ace muttered under his breath.

Will walked up to me and tousled my hair. "You look like you just got out of prison."

"How'd you know? That's exactly what I was going for," I said.

Will looked at me and nodded. "I like it," he declared after a moment's consideration. The first bell rang, so we all scattered to our lockers and classes.

"I just want you to know that I think your hair is complete genius," Alice Leeds, the girl who had helped me open my locker, said to me as I was fishing out my precalculus book.

"Thanks."

As her locker was only two to the left of mine, I usually saw her several times a day. After third period, Alice brought up my hair again. "It's weird, but I can't stop thinking about your hair. It intrigues me. It's like you have nothing to hide behind anymore."

"Um, okay."

At lunch, Alice came up to my table in the cafeteria and handed me a flyer. "I know you're big into yearbook, but I'm directing this play. Come audition, if you want."

I looked at the paper, which announced auditions for the Thomas Purdue Country Day School's production of *Rosencrantz and Guildenstern Are Dead*. "Oh, that's not really my type of thing," I demurred.

"Have you ever been in a play before?" she asked.

"Not since second grade. I played the dual roles of Corn and Plymouth Rock in the school's Thanksgiving pageant. I was pretty awesome."

"Well, if you've really never been in a play, how do you know for sure that it's not your thing?"

By now, Alice was starting to attract the attention of the other people at Ace's table.

"Yeah, Nomi, how do you know?" asked that awful Brianna-girl. Since that first day, she hadn't spoken to me at all unless it was to say something nasty. She really let loose when Ace wasn't there, which he hadn't been that day on account of making up a Spanish test.

"You're right. I don't know. I'll see you there, Alice." I wasn't really going to go. I only said I would because Brianna was being such a jerk.

Alice smiled at me and nodded.

"Nice gloves," Brianna called to Alice as she walked away. Alice was wearing black lace gloves with the fingers cut off. "You better watch out. I heard she's a total lezzie," Brianna whispered.

"What's that supposed to mean?"

"Your hair," she said, sweet as vomit. "It might give some people the wrong idea."

"Your comments might give some people the wrong idea, too," I said even sweeter. I picked up my tray and left. I decided to tell Ace I wasn't ever going to eat with those people again.

Somehow, that day managed to become the best one of school so far. It made me cheerful not to be recognized. I went through my classes in a sort of happy fog and by the time eighth period rolled around, I had completely forgotten about my Advanced Photography Workshop project proposal. Mr. Weir had already given me two other extensions, but for whatever reason, I couldn't come up with an idea. I was probably going to have to drop the class after all.

"So what's it gonna be, Naomi?" Mr. Weir asked.

"Well, it's still in progress," I said, looking around the classroom desperately. Student and professional artwork covered almost every space. In the uppermost corner of the room was a picture from an ultrasound machine. "Maybe something to do with pregnancy?" I suggested.

"Good, but how is that a personal story?" Mr. Weir asked.

"Well . . ." I tried to improvise. "I'm adopted . . . and my sister isn't . . . Is there anything there?"

Mr. Weir thought about it for a second and then nodded. "Maybe. I'd need to hear a bit more first."

I wouldn't have gone to the audition except that I ran into Alice Leeds at our lockers. "Want to walk down with me?" she asked.

And I would have probably said no to that, too, except that idiotic Brianna was watching us from across the hallway. "Sure," I said loudly enough for her to hear. "Let's go."

Alice appraised me over her glasses. "You definitely shouldn't audition for Rosencrantz or Guildenstern. Not with yearbook. Those roles rehearse every day."

"Um, okay."

"I think you might make a good Hamlet . . . I like the idea of a girl Hamlet, don't you?"

"Sure," I said. "Why not?" I watched her make a note on a legal pad and wondered when I could slip out of the theater without her seeing.

At that point, we were inside the theater, and Alice turned her attention to organizing the auditions. I probably could have left, but something kept me there. With its dingy red velvet seats and its scuffed wooden stage, the theater reminded me of a foreign country. It was like all of a sudden discovering that Prague or Berlin was in the middle of my high school. The room was overflowing with nervous energy and excitement, and I guess I wanted to see how it would all turn out.

Before the auditions, Alice made a speech, a few words about the play and her "vision" for it. I liked how passionate she was about things, and somehow she made me forget that I had intended to leave.

As I was at the top of Alice's list, I was the first to read. I guess because I didn't much care whether I was cast or not, it was pretty painless. I even got a few laughs. Whether they were a result of my incompetence or my comedic skills, I couldn't have told you.

I rushed up to the yearbook room. By that time, I was about twenty-five minutes late, and yearbook was in full swing. Without even talking to Will or anyone else, I set down my bag and went immediately to work going through the foreign language clubs' group photos.

"I like that one," Will said, pointing to a picture of the Spanish Honor Society in sombreros. "Better than just a bunch of kids standing around."

I nodded. I had already selected that one myself.

"Maybe all the foreign language club group photos could have themes? Like French in berets?"

"*Oui*. Eating French toast."

"And French fries. Very culturally sensitive and subtle."

"Or how about the sign-language club dressed up like Helen Keller?" I joked.

"Or the Latin club in a graveyard. You know, 'cause it's a dead language?"

I rolled my eyes.

"Yeah, that last one's too gimmicky. I like Helen Keller, though.

Why don't you get on that, Chief? How exactly does one dress up like Helen Keller anyway?"

"Blindfolds? Ear muffs?" I shrugged and went back to going over the pictures.

"Why were you late?" Will asked.

I was about to tell him the story, pass it off like a big joke, but at the last second I didn't. Even though he hadn't been anything but nice, I wanted it to be my own secret, something Will didn't know about me. I doubted I would even get cast in the play anyway, but I wasn't ready to laugh about it yet either. "Mr. Weir kept me after class," I lied.

"Still haven't come up with your project?"

I shook my head.

Sunday night around nine, a girl called me on my cell. Her voice was familiar, but I couldn't quite place it. "Cookie," she said, "what's the story? Are you in or are you out?"

"In, I guess?" In my opinion, it is always better to be in if someone gives you the choice. But actually I had no idea what the girl was talking about.

"Cookie, do you even know who this is?"

"No," I admitted, but that had been happening to me pretty much all the time. I was learning to go with whatever.

"It's Alice Leeds, the director of *Rosencrantz and Guildenstern Are Dead*, and I need to know if you're my pretty girl Hamlet," she said.

"But, Alice, I don't really know the first thing about acting."

Alice didn't care. "These drama kids have so many bad habits, which I need to break them of anyway. You're a virgin, and that's what I like about you. So come be in the play, dolly, it'll be divine, I swear."

Even though I knew Will would probably murder me, I found myself saying yes.

Play rehearsals started the following Monday, which gave me many opportunities to confess to Will. I didn't. Instead, I told him that Dad was now making me see a therapist every Monday and Wednesday after school (I was already wasting my time with that every other Tuesday night), and that he shouldn't expect me until around five on either of those days.

Rehearsals began with everyone in the cast saying their name and the part they would be playing. Next, Alice introduced the crew, which included her assistant, a wardrobe girl (Yvette Schumacher, Estragon from English), the lighting and scenic designers, and others. The very last person Alice introduced was James Larkin, who was designing the video installation to accompany the play and who took no notice of me at all. I wasn't completely sure what "designing the video installation" meant, but I had no intention of asking him either. James had made it perfectly clear that whatever had happened between us in the hospital was just about him being a Good Samaritan, nothing more.

We read through the play. I had more lines than I had been expecting.

After that, Yvette measured me for my costume. While she worked, I watched Alice and James having a discussion across the theater. "That new guy is scorching," Yvette said. "Totally Alice's type. I should be jealous."

"Jealous of James?" I asked.

"No, silly, Alice," she said. "She's my"—she lowered her voice—"girlfriend, but she likes boys, too. I don't know why I'm whispering. It's not exactly a secret."

Of course, everything was a secret to me.

"How long have you and Alice been together?" I asked.

"Just since the beginning of last summer. She's been my best friend since third grade, but it was extremely tortured for a while. It took us forever to admit anything to each other."

Rehearsal was over just before six. As I was walking out, Alice called me over. "Naomi, cookie, come and meet James!"

James said, "We've met before." He studied me. "Her hair was different then."

At his mention of my hair, I felt self-conscious and reached up to play with it.

"Don't listen to him. It's brilliant," Alice said. "I never would have thought of you for the part if you hadn't done it. She looks just like that actress from the French movie, I can't remember her name."

"Jean Seberg," James said. "*A bout de souffle*. In English, *Breathless*. Directed by Jean-Luc Godard. 1960. The film that started the nouvelle vague. My second favorite Godard film. It'd probably be my favorite Godard except that it's everyone's favorite, so my first is *2 or 3 Things I Know About Her*."

"James is a movie buff," Alice reported, despite it being perfectly evident.

"And Jean wasn't French, she was American," James said. "Not to mention, your hair is darker than hers. Incidentally, I didn't say it was different in a bad way." He cocked his head lazily and squinted at me. "I like it better now."

"Well, now that that's out of the way," Alice said, clapping her hands. "You'll be working together." She explained that it was her intention that Hamlet's story be an important part of the video projections. "You both should get started as soon as possible," Alice said.

James asked me if I needed a ride. He suggested we sort out our schedules on the way home. His car was out of the shop.

Even though I'd been planning to go upstairs to *The Phoenix* to work, I found myself saying yes.

During the short ride to my house, we figured out that Saturday afternoon was the best time for both of us (he worked Saturday and Sunday nights), and before I knew it, he was pulling into my driveway.

"Hey," I said, "how did you know where I lived?"

"*That* is a good question," he said.

I waited for him to continue, but he didn't, so I asked him *why* it was a good question.

"The thing is, I looked it up. I thought I might stop by your house to see how you were doing."

"But you didn't?"

"Guess not."

I considered saying how I wished he had, but then Ace's face popped into my head. For better or worse, Ace was still my boyfriend, so it didn't seem right for me to be flirting with some other guy, particularly one who ran as hot and cold as James.

Instead, I told James that I would see him on Saturday and got out of the car.

Later that night, I was on the phone with Ace. "But what about homecoming?" he asked. The dance was also that Saturday, and we had planned to go with Brianna and her boyfriend, Alex. Alex had been one of Ace's best tennis team buddies before he graduated and went to NYU.

I assured him that it was fine. "I'll be done with play stuff around five." I decided not to mention James.

"Is that gonna give you enough time?" Ace asked.

"What do you know about it?" I countered.

"I do have a sister, Naomi. All that girl stuff takes serious prep."

"How long does it take to put on a dress?" I asked.

"I wouldn't know. What about your makeup? Your nails?"

"You worried I'm gonna be ugly, Ace?" I teased him.

"Guess you won't be needing much time for your hair."

"Ha," I said.

James picked me up on Saturday at noon. When I got outside, I could see that Yvette was sitting in the front seat of his mom's station wagon, and in the backseat was a suitcase full of period costumes. I hadn't known she was coming.

Once I was in the car, Yvette turned around to look at me. "James and Alice thought it would be cool if you played Ophelia and Hamlet in the projections, so I've got costumes for both. And a wig for the Ophelia part."

We drove to a park a couple of towns over in Rye. And James videoed me standing on a rock in a Hamlet costume, and then lying soaked in a river as Ophelia, and the day pretty much went like that until a ranger came to kick us out of the park because we didn't have the proper permits for shooting video. James reasoned with the guy and said since we were students we didn't need permits, and the ranger said we could stay fifteen minutes longer. This was fine with me; I was completely freezing and had been all day. Even though I hadn't complained, James remembered about my being cold and made sure that Yvette covered me up with a coat whenever we weren't shooting. James was really professional that way. I'd seen my mom at work, and he reminded me a little of her.

Back in the car, Yvette said she had to go get ready for home-coming. She was going with Alice and a group of girls from drama. James said he would drop her off first and me second. On the way to her house, Yvette teased James about not going to homecoming. "Just about everybody in the play asked him, you know. Girls *and* boys," she said to me.

James laughed. He said that not *everyone* had asked him and that he had to work anyway.

When we reached Yvette's house, James and I helped her take all the costumes inside. She kissed James on the cheek. My involuntary and embarrassing reaction was to wonder if I could get away with doing that same thing when we got to my house.

Yvette kissed me on the cheek, too. "Maybe I'll see you tonight, doll," she said.

On the drive to my house, James asked me if I was going to the dance that night. I told him that I was, "With Ace."

"Ah yes, the jock. Good name for a tennis player, Ace is."

"Unless you've got a run of bad serves," I joked.

James didn't laugh, but then it hadn't been much of a joke, I suppose.

About a minute later, he said, "You were good out there today. Really game and relaxed. You made things easy for me. You're amazing at keeping still."

I laughed. "What can I say? It's a gift." I told him how my mom had been a photographer, so I had spent most of my life posing for one thing or another.

"Had been?"

"Well, still is. But we're not really speaking at the moment."

He didn't push me to say anything more about my mother, which I appreciated. "I don't know a thing about acting, so that probably accounts for my relaxation," I said.

"Maybe you should just accept the compliment," he said.

But I'd never been much good there. At least not that I could remember. "Where do you work?" I asked.

He told me that he worked at the community college as an AV specialist, which basically meant projecting movies and videos for their adult education classes. "Pays pretty well, and my dad thinks I ought to have a job. I get to watch a lot of things I wouldn't otherwise get to see."

"Like what?"

"Oh, over the summer, there was this class on Swedish cinema, so I've pretty much watched everything Bergman ever did. Do you know who Ingmar Bergman is?"

I shook my head.

"He's this brilliant director. His films are mainly about sex and memory. You'd probably find them interesting with . . . well, everything that's happened to you," he said. "And now there's this class about the films of Woody Allen, so I've been watching a lot of his, too. I like him, but not as much as Bergman."

"I love Woody," I said. "My parents used to always rent all his movies when I was little. I especially love *Hannah and Her Sisters* and

The Purple Rose of Cairo." I was glad that there were some things I could still remember liking.

"Maybe you could come down sometime and watch a couple?" he suggested. "I could get you in. Not that it's any big thing. You could bring your jock." I'm pretty sure he was teasing me with that last part, but his deadpan made it hard to tell.

By then, he was pulling into my driveway. I told him that I doubted that Ace even liked Woody.

"Probably not," he said. "Have a good time at your dance, Naomi."

I wore the black velvet dress from my closet because I hadn't had time to buy anything else. (Maybe the truth was that I hadn't *made* time to buy anything else.) At the very least, *I* couldn't remember having worn it before.

"Even better than last year," Dad said when I came downstairs.

When he came to pick me up, Ace didn't mention my having worn the dress before. He just kissed me on the cheek. "You look nice."

Ace drove us all to the dance. I sat in front with him, and Brianna sat in the backseat with Alex, who, despite being Ace's good friend, turned out to be a complete dick. I actually felt sorry for Brianna, which was saying something. The boy was drunk before we even left for the dance, and he kept trying to kiss her and paw her. I kept hearing her say, "No, Alex. No. Just wait, would you?" and other things like that. Ace turned up the radio, I think, to give them privacy, but maybe he was simply tired of listening to Brianna's protests.

Finally, I turned around and said, "Look, Alex, hold off for fifteen minutes, will you? She wants to look nice for her picture, okay?"

"Naomi, it's fine," Brianna said icily.

I tried to make a joke of it. "She probably spent the last ten years getting ready."

I think I heard Alex mumble something about "immature high school kids," but I wasn't sure.

The rest of the car ride was completely silent. I could tell Brianna, Ace, and that tool Alex were all pissed at me. I didn't care about Brianna or Alex, but I felt somewhat bad about Ace. I started to regret having said anything in the first place. I mean, a girl like Brianna could take care of herself.

Inside the dance, they named the homecoming king and queen, and I saw one of the freshman staffers from yearbook taking pictures. I could tell that the pictures weren't going to turn out well. For one, the angle was too low, which would give everyone double chins, and for two, he wasn't getting any sort of variety. I went over to him and told him to stand on the table. He did. Then he thanked me and said that he was getting better stuff. He showed me a few in his camera's digital monitor. I took off my heels and got on the table and shot a couple of frames myself. It was the most fun I'd had all night. I started to hypothesize that maybe the reason I had gotten so involved with yearbook was because I had liked taking pictures. Maybe it had been that simple. I wondered if it was *all* that simple—if my memory never came back, maybe it was as easy as asking myself what I liked and what I didn't like.

When I turned to get off the table, Will was standing under me. "Can I help?" he asked, offering me his hand.

I accepted it. It's difficult to get off a table in a dress.

"I didn't think you were coming."

"I wasn't planning on it. I despise these things. Patten got sick, so I had to cover the photo keychain booth." The photo keychain booth was one of yearbook's many fundraisers. "Your dress—" Will began.

"I know, I know. It's the same one I wore last year."

"If you'd let me finish, I was going to say that it looks better with your hair that way," he said. "You clean up good, Chief."

"Thanks." I slipped my heels back on, and I was now looking down at Will a spike's worth. "I like your suit," I told him.

"Had to improvise." He was wearing an emerald velvet suit and a paisley shirt. He was the only person dressed even remotely that way. "Get any good homecoming court pictures?" he asked.

I rolled my eyes. "Just your usual thrill of victory, agony of defeat."

"Ah, youth. Bittersweet. Fleeting," he wisecracked.

"Exactly."

"I watched you, though," Will said, looking me right in the eye. "You looked really, really . . . happy up there."

I had been happy, but I didn't like the way Will was looking at me. No, *looking* isn't the right word. *Seeing*. I wasn't comfortable with how much Will saw. He made me feel transparent when I was still opaque to myself.

He said he'd tried calling me that afternoon, but that my phone had been off. I was about to make up yet another lie when Ace was suddenly by my side. "Will," Ace said.

Will nodded. "Zuckerman."

"Been harassing my girl?" Ace said, putting his arm around me.

I knew that objectively speaking there was nothing wrong with Ace calling me "his girl," and yet the arm offended me. It seemed over the top. "Just yearbook business," I said.

"Right. Always with the yearbook business," Ace said in a nasty tone that perplexed me.

"Yeah, how else are we going to preserve your glory years, Zuckerman?" Will asked.

I felt like I didn't know quite what was going on between Ace and Will. Somehow, it made me long for James.

"So, Will, you mind if I take my girl for a dance?"

"She doesn't like to dance," Will said under his breath. Then he excused himself. I didn't see him for the rest of the night.

After the dance, Brianna and Alex decided to get a ride home with someone else, so Ace and I were alone in the car. I thought he was just driving me back to my house, but instead he took me to his.

He said his parents had gone to Boston for the weekend and that we had the run of the place.

He asked me if I wanted a drink, and I declined. I had been avoiding alcohol since his friend's party, which seemed like something he might have guessed.

He led me to his room, which was tidy and preppy like the rest of the house, and like Ace himself, for that matter. The wallpaper was plaid, and vintage wooden tennis rackets hung from the wall. I looked at his bookshelves, and other than school books all he had were athletes' memoirs and a set of leather-bound classics. He had one picture of us taped to the wall by his bed. We were both dressed for tennis. The picture was out of focus, but I could see my hair was in a ponytail, the way Ace had said that he liked me best.

I sat down on his bed: an old, spring-loaded mattress that sounded like it was wheezing. Ace sat down next to me—*squeak*—and kissed me on the mouth. He still tasted like Gatorade even though I knew for a fact he hadn't had any for at least the last five hours.

"Do you remember what happened here a year ago?" he asked.

Duh, I had amnesia. "No," I said.

So he told me. At last year's homecoming dance, Ace and I had "put one over the net"—i.e., we had done it for the first time. We had "played several sets" since then, but had mutually agreed to sit out the "summer season" for reasons which Ace chose not to specify. It was his idea that we should celebrate our anniversary with a "rematch." I'm not sure if nerves were the reason for Ace's lame sports/sex metaphors, but it was starting to put the whole tennis wristbands debacle into pathetic perspective.

I told him that I still hadn't started up with the pill again, and he said, "That's okay. I've come equipped." He whipped out a pack of condoms from the nightstand like a sports manager providing balls for the team. His hands were so quick—I barely saw him open or close the drawer—I got a sense of what he was probably like on the courts.

I felt oddly numb about the whole thing. My thinking was along the lines of *Well, I've done it before. Might as well get it over with and do it again.*

Ace started to unzip my dress, but he couldn't get the zipper down. "This is stuck," he said.

"Well, don't break it," I protested. "I need to be able to put it back on."

At that moment, his one-hundred-year-old basset hound came into the room to say hello. "Get, Jonesy," Ace said. "Get!"

Jonesy didn't want to go. He mounted Ace's right leg and started humping it. Ace kept shaking his leg at Jonesy, but the dog would not be deterred. "Get, get!" Ace stood up and pushed Jonesy from the room, but I could still hear the dog's howls outside the door.

I started to laugh. It struck me as humorous that something Ace didn't want his dog to do was something he desperately wanted me to do.

"Where were we?" Ace asked.

The whole thing was absurd.

Since I couldn't remember the "real" first time I'd lost my virginity, this would have become my de facto first time. I wanted a better story than *I did it with this boy who I wasn't very into and who had mysterious Gatorade breath; in his room decorated with sports equipment; at least he was nice enough to provide condoms and get his ancient, horny dog to leave us alone.* Put it that way, and I couldn't help but wonder how I'd let it get so far in the first place.

"Ace, I'm not going to have sex with you," I said. I reached over my shoulder and zipped my dress back up without any problems.

"Is it the howls? I can put the dog in the yard," Ace said. "Just hold on a second. I can get him to stop. Bad Jonesy! Bad dog."

I told him that it wasn't about the dog.

"Well, what is it then?" He walked over to his bedroom window. His back was toward me, and I couldn't see his face.

"I . . . I just don't know," I said. "The truth is, I don't even know you. I don't even know what we have in common."

"There's lots of stuff," Ace said.

"Tell me, then. I'd really like to know."

"Tennis. School." Ace sighed. He wouldn't turn back around. "I love you, Naomi."

"Why?"

He shrugged violently. "Jesus, I don't know. Why does anyone like anyone? Because you're super-hot?"

"Are you asking me or telling me?"

"I'm asking you. I mean I'm telling you. I don't know. You're confusing me." Ace turned around and looked at me helplessly, hopelessly. "Because you're good at school, but can also hold a drink. Because we used to talk about stuff. I don't know. I just did."

"Did or do?"

"What's that supposed to mean?"

"*Did* in the past, or *do* in the present?"

"Do! I meant do. Isn't that what I said?" He collapsed onto his bed, so that he was staring up at his ceiling. The box spring squeaked in agony, which started Jonesy barking again. I opened Ace's door, and Jonesy ran in. Luckily, Jonesy wasn't in the mood for sex anymore either. He wanted cuddling and intimacy. He jumped onto the bed and lay down next to Ace.

"But honestly, you've been acting so weird lately," Ace said quietly.

Maybe because I can't remember anything? I thought bitterly.

"Like yelling at Alex in the car, what was that about? And now you're in this play? And your hair!"

It was the first he'd mentioned it since the day I'd cut it. I had no idea he was still thinking about it. "What about my hair?" I asked. Not because I cared, but because I was sort of curious.

"I loved it long."

It was the second time he'd used the word love all night, but it was the only time I believed him.

"I'm not used to it this way," he continued. "I honestly don't even know what to think."

"Say what you mean, Ace."

"I *hate* your stupid hair," he said, his voice rusty with truth, bitterness, feeling. Everything else he'd said the whole time we'd been together had sounded merely confused or frustrated, but this was different. This was unmistakable. This was passion! It was what was missing from every other element of my relationship with Ace. It was what I'd heard when Alice spoke about the play, or Will about yearbook, or Dad about Rosa Rivera. It was what I'd heard when James had said he'd wanted to kiss me in the hospital.

For the record, I didn't know boys could care so much about hair. Maybe this was asking too much, but I wanted someone who felt as strongly about the rest of me. Poor Ace. The boy had been in love with a haircut.

I knew what I had to do.

"I think we should take some time off. From each other, I mean," I said. Then I tried to make a joke. "Give my hair some time to grow."

Ace didn't laugh. "Are you saying you want to break up?" he asked. Did I detect a hint of relief in his voice?

"Yes."

"But that's not what I want!" Ace protested a little too adamantly. "I want you to get your memory back and for everything to be like it was."

"Well, maybe that will happen. But in all likelihood, it won't. And you'll be in college next year anyway, so this was bound to happen sooner or later," I reasoned.

"Is it Will?" Ace asked.

This annoyed me. It only confirmed how much Ace didn't know me. If anyone, it was James, and it wasn't even James. It was no one. Or, more to the point, no one except Ace. "Will's my friend, which is more than I can say for you."

Ace closed his eyes. "This wasn't the way I saw tonight going."

I asked him if he could drive me home. When we got to my house, he walked me to the door. I kissed him on the cheek.

"I know this is probably dumb, but I feel like I'm never going to see you again," he said.

"Don't be ridiculous, Ace. I'll see you at school," I replied, but of course I knew exactly what he had meant.

"What I said about your hair . . ." he began.

"It's okay. You were being honest."

By the following Tuesday, everyone at school seemed to know about our breakup. The story got back to me that Ace had dumped me because I was a "prude" in bed since the accident and "not entirely there," both of which had some basis in truth while not conveying the essential nature of what had happened. I didn't know if Ace spread these rumors or if they were just the idle speculation of my peers. People like Brianna, who'd had it in for me even more since I'd tried to stand up for her in the car. She could really let loose now that Ace was no longer required to defend my honor.

I would have understood if it had been Ace—maybe he was saving face, or maybe that was how he actually saw things? In any case, I did not go out of my way to set the record straight. People could think what they wanted to. Screw them.

Six

I STILL HADN'T TOLD WILL ABOUT THE PLAY. Maybe it was because I felt like I was betraying him; maybe it was plain cowardice. I was late to yearbook about half the time and I let him think I was either with tutors or at the doctor. If my chronic tardiness annoyed him, Will was too much of a friend to let on.

He probably wouldn't have found out about it at all, if Bailey Plotkin hadn't shown up to photograph rehearsals. Bailey was the arts photographer for *The Phoenix*, the same position I'd held my freshman year, according to that year's masthead. If I'd been paying any attention to yearbook matters, I might have guessed someone from the staff would eventually come.

Bailey was a mellow person in general, and he didn't appear particularly surprised to see me. "I didn't know you were in the play, Naomi. Cool," was pretty much all he said about the matter. Still, I knew I had to tell Will, and preferably before he saw the pictures.

I went to the yearbook office as soon as rehearsal was over, and Will barely glanced up at me when I came into the room. He asked me if I'd had time to look over the cover mock-ups. I hadn't, so I went to do that. The cover Will liked was all white with just the words *The Phoenix* in raised black text, all caps, right justified, halfway down the page. It was extremely plain and not the sort of thing you usually see on a high school yearbook. He had mentioned that it was a reference to an album or a book, but I hadn't been paying enough attention. I wasn't sure how I felt about it yet.

For the next two hours until yearbook was over, Will said nothing to me about the play. He was all business the whole time: very polite questions and no wisecracks. This was unlike him and only confirmed my belief that he already knew but was waiting for me to bring it up.

At the end of the meeting, I asked him for a ride home. "So that we can talk," I added. He was quiet on the walk out to the parking lot. It was the end of October and I felt a chill, but it wasn't from the weather. That fall had been particularly mild, and I was wearing a hoodie and a parka besides. I think the chill might have been something like déjà vu. I felt as if I had taken this very same walk before. Of course, I had. I had gotten many rides from Will since I'd been back at school, but there was something specifically familiar that I couldn't quite identify.

"Are you cold?" he asked me when we were halfway to the parking lot. "I should have offered you my gloves."

I shook my head. Will was always so concerned about me—even now, when he likely knew I'd been lying to him for weeks. It made me feel like the smallest person in the world.

When we got to the car, he stood there for a second without unlocking the doors.

"So?" I said.

"So, you're the one who wanted to talk, Chief."

"Well, um, in the car's fine," I said.

"I'd rather hear it here," Will said.

I told him. "I'm in the play. I don't know why I didn't mention it before. That thing about the additional therapy was a lie." I glanced over the roof of his car to see his reaction. He didn't have one really, so I rambled on. "It happened almost by accident," I continued, "but it's only another two weeks, and then I'll be back full-time."

Will nodded for a second before replying, "You had sure as hell better comp me, Chief." He loosened his school tie and then he laughed, so I asked him what was funny. "The thing is, I'd been afraid you were going to quit."

"Why?"

"For the last couple of weeks, we've barely spoken. At least now I know there was a reason."

I assumed he meant the play.

"And your heart hasn't really been in it for a while. It's only natural that I wondered. I want you to know I would probably have understood if you *had* quit with everything that's happened to you, but I'm relieved that you didn't."

Will unlocked the doors to his car and we got in.

"The play . . . is it fun?" he asked me.

"Yeah, it is," I admitted.

"I'm glad." Will nodded and then he started the car.

When he got to my house, he asked if he could come in. He said he hadn't seen my dad in a while.

I asked him why in the world he wanted to see my dad.

"Well, I really like his books. We're pals, Grant and me."

I told him that Dad was probably writing.

"Come on, Chief," he said. "I haven't been over to your house in eons."

We went inside, but Dad wasn't even there. Instead of leaving, Will sat down at the kitchen table. "I heard you and Zuckerman broke up," he said.

"Yeah." I didn't really want to talk about it with Will, but he wasn't taking the hint.

"Why?" Will asked.

"Because he hated my hair," I said.

"I always thought he was a dick," Will said.

"A dick?"

Will blushed for a second. "Maybe not a dick, but not good enough for you."

"He's okay."

"Is there somebody else?" Will asked. He took off his glasses and wiped them on his pants.

"Nope," I said. "I'm not planning on it either."

He said he didn't believe me.

"Well, you can believe what you want. But I've got enough on my plate without a boy." Then I told Will I needed to study, which was true.

I'd finally gotten him to the front door when he spun around and said, "You know how I call you 'Chief'?"

I nodded.

"Didn't you ever wonder what you call me?"

"Uh, 'Will'?"

"No, what you used to call me."

I hadn't.

"Coach. You know, short for *co-chief*. You could call me that again if you wanted to, Chief. If it ever should happen to just pop into your head."

"Coach," I said. Despite the fact that he couldn't have been less athletic, the nickname suited him well. A good nickname tells you something about the person it belongs to, and it was so with this one. In all he did, Will was fiercely loyal, a good motivator, intelligent, passionate, and thoughtful. He was everything a coach ought to be. "It's a good name for you," I said. "I wish I'd thought to ask you about it before."

"There are all sorts of things I could tell you," he said, "if you ever wanted to know them."

The play opened the second weekend in November. Each of the cast members was allotted four tickets. I gave one to Will and two to Dad, who gave one to Rosa Rivera. I thought about giving my last ticket to Mom, but my part wasn't all that big for her to bother driving in from the city. Plus, I didn't have enough tickets for Nigel and their kid anyway.

The show ran for only two nights, so in a way it wasn't all that different from yearbook—a lot of effort for not much product. But, well, I think it was a good play. That must count for something. Will, his mother, Dad, and Rosa Rivera came on the second night, and everyone told me it was a good play, and that I was good in it. I was really only in a couple of scenes. To commemorate the occasion, Will made me a new mix CD, *Songs for Acting Like You're at Your Therapist When You're Really Just Acting* ("Hilarious," I said), which he gave me after the show was over; I hadn't finished listening to his last mix yet. Dad said how he liked the video installation part that James had done. The footage *had* looked pretty amazing projected—you would never have known that we shot it at a park in Rye. James had treated the footage so that it looked like an old silent movie. All black-and-white and faded and flickery.

The cast party was at Alice's house. Or behind Alice's house by her pool. It being November, the pool was covered over with a green vinyl tarp.

Yvette hugged and congratulated me. In return, I told her how amazing the costumes had looked. "Have you seen James?" she asked.

"Why?"

"I didn't get a chance to tell him how beautiful his images were. Best part of the play. Don't tell Alice," she whispered.

I swore that I wouldn't.

I hadn't encountered James since that day at the park. He didn't need to go to actor rehearsals, and at the few rehearsals he did attend, he was occupied with technical matters. Truthfully, I had been too busy to care. Besides, I was past expecting that anything might happen between us.

Alice came up to me next. "Where's your cocktail, cookie?" This was the drama crowd—while there was no beer, there was plenty of harder stuff.

"I'm abstaining," I said.

"Do you have a problem with drinking?" Alice asked me.

"Yes. I have no tolerance to an embarrassing degree." No one really wants to hear about your medical problems at a party.

Alice laughed. "Sounds like it'd be fun to get you liquored up, cookie."

I just shook my head.

Alice kissed me on both cheeks and told me she was so proud of me. And then the guy who had played Guildenstern called her. "Who do you think is cuter? Rosencrantz or Guildenstern?" Alice asked. "I simply can't decide who I prefer."

"What about Yvette?" I asked her.

"Yvette, Yvette, sweet Yvette." Alice sighed heavily. We both turned to watch Yvette, who was laughing with another girl in the play. "We are in high school, and that means I don't have to marry anybody."

My curfew was midnight, and I was about to get a ride home with the doomed Yvette, who like most doomed people seemed to have no clue, when someone tapped me on the shoulder. "Hey, Hamlet," James said.

"You're late," I replied.

He shrugged. "I didn't think I was going to come." He took a cigarette out of his jacket and lit it.

"Aren't you gonna offer me one?" I asked.

"I would, but I didn't think you smoked."

"Still, it's nice to be asked. Courtesy, you know?"

"Truthfully"—James inhaled deeply, and his gray eyes were lit by the flame from his cigarette—"truthfully I don't want to be the guy who ruins your pretty pink lungs."

It sounded an awful lot like flirting. I'd been down that road with James before, and it never led anywhere.

I said that I had to go home. He offered to drive me, but I told him that Yvette was driving me. "In case I don't see you again," I said, "I just wanted to say that I thought the installation was beautiful."

James tossed off my praise. "Yeah, turned out pretty decent. I'm only doing this play thing to have something extra to put on my college applications in case my first choice doesn't work out."

"Well, it doesn't matter why," I said. "It was beautiful anyhow." I turned to leave.

He finished his cigarette in a single inhale. "Wait a second. Don't I get to compliment you, too?"

I shook my head and told him it was too late for that. "I'd probably assume it was in response to mine."

"I was afraid of that," he said.

"It was nice seeing you, James." I pointed him in the direction of the drinks and the partygoers with curfews later than mine.

"I don't drink. I mean, I used to. But not anymore," he said. "And besides, the person I came to see was you. You remember that class I told you about?"

I did.

"They're showing *Hannah and Her Sisters* on Tuesday night. You said that was one of your favorites, right?" he said. "It's cool if you bring the jock, too. Do you have a piece of paper?" I held out my hand, palm facing out, and he took a black Sharpie from his pocket and wrote the screening information on my palm.

I had no intention of going. The play had made me fall farther behind in my schoolwork, and I had yearbook, and James did not seem like a good bet for a boyfriend or even a friend, not that I was looking for either. In fact, I tried to wash his note from my hand that night before bed, but those Sharpies really have staying power, even on skin. Tuesday rolled around, and as I could still see it, ever so slightly, I decided what the hell.

Dad dropped me off, and he told me to call him when the movie was done. It was a pain not to be able to drive myself places, but I didn't really have time to take driving lessons until the summer.

It seemed to me that every senior citizen in Tarrytown was there. Having seen the movie before, I didn't have to pay too much attention to it, which was lucky, because the old people made quite a lot of noise unwrapping candies and whispering to each other, *What did she just say?* I found myself thinking of the last time I'd seen it with Mom. Mom's favorite part was when this guy tells this woman (not Hannah, one of the sisters) to read a certain page of a book because it had a line of poetry on it that reminded him of her. The line was "No one, not even the rain, has such soft hands," or something like that, and it always made Mom cry. I wondered if Nigel had done stuff like that for Mom, and if that's why she'd left Dad for him.

The movie ended, and I decided to wait for James to come out of the projection booth, just to be polite.

When he finally emerged, he asked me how I had liked seeing the movie again.

I guess I was still thinking about Mom, because I found myself telling him all about Dad and Mom and Nigel. How I kind of wished Mom had seen the play, because she really got a kick out of that sort of thing. How I kind of wanted to see her, but I didn't know how to do it without making a big production of it. The horrible name I'd called her the last time I'd seen her—

James cut me off. "None of that matters. If you want to see her, you should go. Take off and do it. Don't wait." He started talking about his brother, and then he cut himself off, too. "Oh, you don't want to hear all my sad stories. I can't even bear to tell them anymore. Screw the past, right?"

Screw the past. It made me so happy to hear someone say that. I felt lighter, like when I first cut my hair.

His gray eyes clouded for a moment, and then he laughed. "Say, Naomi, there's something real serious I've been meaning to ask you," he said, his voice suddenly filled with gravity again.

"What?"

He grinned. "Whatever happened to that shirt I lent you?"

The dress shirt was hanging in my closet at home. "I washed it," I told him. "Come get it now, if you'd like."

Dad was locked away in his office working when we got there.

"Do you want to meet my dad?" I whispered.

"I've already met him," James reminded me. "In the hospital."

"Right. I'm sure he'd like to thank you, though."

"Next time," James said shyly. "I don't always go over so well with people's parents."

I led James to my room and located his shirt in the back of my closet. As I handed it to him, my hand brushed up against his forearm, but James didn't seem to notice.

"Thanks," he said.

We were both standing in the entrance to my closet, which was a walk-in. James was looking around when he said, "What is that?" He pointed to a stack of CliffsNotes on the top shelf.

"I know. It's very scandalous. In my defense, I can't remember buying them."

James set down his shirt and took the top booklet off the stack. "*Slaughterhouse Five*. For God's sake, who buys CliffsNotes to *Slaughterhouse Five*."

"Apparently that was the kind of girl I was."

"The very bad kind," James said. He picked up his shirt and moved to leave my closet.

James had run hot and cold in the months since I had met him, so I'm not exactly sure what possessed me to do what I did next. They say that people who have had brain injuries sometimes suffer from strange emotional outbursts, and I guess this would qualify. "Do you remember what you asked me back at the hospital?"

He didn't answer.

"When my dad came in?"

He still didn't answer.

"About kissing me and if you had permission?"

"Yeah," he said in a low voice, "I remember."

"Well, you would have had it." I took a deep breath, and then I added, "I'm not with Ace anymore."

He took my hand in his and said, "Naomi, don't you think I knew that?"

Then I kissed James, or he kissed me.

(Who knows how these things start?)

And then I kissed James again, or he kissed me again.

(And if you don't know who started it, it's hard to know what came next.)

And I and him, and him and me.

(I will always remember that he tasted like cigarettes and something passing sweet, which I could not quite identify.)

Andiandhimandhimandme.

(And so on.)

It might have gone on like that forever except that Dad knocked on my door. "Kiddo?"

James and I broke apart, and I told Dad to come in.

"I didn't know you had company," Dad said.

"I don't, not really. James just stopped by to pick something up, and I didn't want to bother you if you were working. You met James at the hospital, remember?" I went on and on. Even though we hadn't been doing it or anything, I knew that that kiss was written all over my face. Also, I couldn't stop smiling.

Dad nodded distractedly. "Oh hey. Yeah." Dad reached over to shake James's hand. "Thanks for all your help, son."

James nodded. "My pleasure. Well, I've got my shirt." James held up the shirt, presumably for Dad's benefit. "Guess I'll be on my way. See you in school, Naomi."

"I'll walk you out," I said.

As I walked James to the door, he whispered to me, "Is that gonna cause trouble for you?"

"My dad's cool." I really didn't care if it did anyway. "Whenever I break one of Dad's rules, I can always claim amnesia."

"I believe you used it with the CliffsNotes, too," James pointed out.

"But—"

"Don't deny it, Naomi. It really is a good, all-purpose excuse. Robbed a bank? 'But, officer, I didn't *remember* I wasn't supposed to rob banks.' I wish I could use that one, too."

"What would you use it for?"

He raised an eyebrow. "Things. Mainly things I'd done in the past, but you never know what might come up."

At the door, he kissed me again.

When I got back to my room, Dad was waiting for me. Of course, he wanted to know if I was seeing James, but I wasn't sure of the answer to that yet. "Not technically."

"He's very handsome, and he looks older than you, if I'm not mistaken. Both of which do not exactly recommend him to me, your dear old dad. I assume you know what you're doing though."

I nodded.

"In any case, I came to talk to you about the wedding." He said that they were planning to have it at a hotel on Martha's Vineyard the second weekend of June. It would just be me and him; Rosa Rivera and her two daughters, her sister, and her brother; Dad's mother, my grandmother Rollie; and "significant others of the aforementioned." He said Rosa Rivera wanted me to be a bridesmaid along with her two daughters, which struck me as ridiculous.

"But, Dad, I barely know the woman!"

"You'd be doing it for me, too."

"Not to mention who'll be left to watch the wedding if nearly everyone's a bridesmaid?"

Dad said that wasn't the point.

"It wasn't that long ago you were lying to me about even having a girlfriend, and now you want me to be in your wedding. It seems fast and unfair, and . . ."

"And?" Dad prompted. "And what?"

I thought of when James had said "screw the past," how right that had felt. I was moving forward with James, and Dad was moving forward with Rosa Rivera, and screw whatever had come before. I was going to be all about *now*, about *am*, about *present tense*. "Tell Rosa Rivera I'm happy to be her bridesmaid."

Dad's stunned look was pleasurable in and of itself. "I thought we were in for the long haul on this one, but I guess not. Don't get me wrong, I'm thrilled, but why the sudden change of heart?"

I felt reckless and happy, so I kissed my father on the cheek. "Oh, Dad, what possible difference can *why* make anyway? Just go with it."

My phone rang. It was Will, so I told Dad I had to take it. Dad just nodded. I could tell he was still dazed by my turnabout. I vowed to do it more often.

"You sound different," Will said skeptically. "Your voice is all full of . . . I don't know what."

I laughed at him. I liked being unpredictable, unreadable.

"It's that cat James," he said simply.

This seemed to come out of nowhere. I hadn't mentioned James to Will since that day we picked him up. "Sort of," I admitted. "What makes you say that?"

"I have eyes, Chief. I saw your play. I read the program. If you're in love, I'm happy for you. You don't have to hide it. He certainly seems more interesting than Zuckerman."

"I'm not in love," I said finally. "I like him."

"There're those rumors about him—"

I interrupted. "I don't care about any of that. It's in the past." It was my new philosophy. It had to be.

"I heard he used to be an addict and that he got thrown out of his old school and sent to—"

"Did you hear me? I said I don't care."

"I'm not gossiping," Will said. "I'm only watching out for my friend. Personally, I think it's better to know more than less. I'm not saying you should listen to any of the crap the kids at Tom Purdue say, but it might be worth addressing with James—"

"Christ, Will, would you stop being such an old man? You're worse than my father," I snapped. "I haven't even gone on a date with James yet."

"Sorry," he said coolly.

"Why are you calling anyway?" I snapped again.

"I don't remember," he said after a pause. "I'll see you at school." He hung up the phone.

I was thinking how Will pulled things backward when what I needed was to be in this moment, now, when my phone rang again. I didn't recognize the number, but I picked up anyway.

It was James.

"Did you get in trouble?"

"Not really."

"Good, because I was thinking I could take you out this Saturday."

Saturday was my seventeenth birthday. I had planned to go out with Dad for dinner, but I could always cancel that. I had dinner with Dad all the time.

"Sounds like a plan," I said.

Dad gave me my present right before James was set to pick me up.

That year, the book he gave me was blank. The cover was made from taupe suede, and a leather cord wrapped around it so that it could be tied shut. The edges of the pages were gilded. He inscribed it "Write your life. Love, Dad." For a variety of reasons, the gift offended me, and I briefly considered throwing it in the trash before just deciding to bury it under my bed among the dust, widowed socks, and other lost things.

Dad asked me what I thought of his selection.

"I would have preferred a novel," I said.

"You didn't like it?"

"I think it's in somewhat bad taste to give an amnesiac a blank book."

Of course, that was what I wanted to say. What I actually said was "It's nice, but I doubt I'll have much time for writing in it." This was true enough, too.

Dad smiled and said, "You will. And you'll want to."

That seemed unlikely. Writing has always seemed such a backward activity to me, and that was most definitely not the direction I wanted to go. When my parents were still the Wandering Porters, I thought of summer as the living time; the rest of the year was the backward time, the writing time.

The doorbell rang, and it was James. He was wearing his corduroy jacket even though it was too light for the season. He was so handsome I nearly wanted to swoon. The word *swoon* had never even popped into my head before I saw him that night, let alone as something that I might do.

He smelled like soap with only the faintest hint of cigarettes. He was holding a wrapped CD, which he handed to me.

"How'd you know it was my birthday?" I asked.

"I didn't. This was sitting on your doorstep. Happy birthday anyway. What is it?"

I tore open the paper. "Just a mix from my friend." The CD liner read: "*Songs for a Teenage Amnesiac, Vol. II: The Motion Picture Soundtrack*, Happy 17th Birthday. I Remain Your Faithful Servant, William B. Landsman." There wasn't even a playlist; he must have run out of time when he was putting it together. I tossed the thing on the bench in the hallway.

"We could listen to it in my car," James suggested.

"Okay." I shrugged. Will usually had good taste in music, and the songs wouldn't mean anything to me anyway.

James put the CD in the car player, but no sound came out. "This player's old, and it can be a little spastic with home-burned stuff." James popped the CD out and handed it back to me. I thought about throwing it out the window; I was still pissed at Will from yesterday. Instead, I just slipped it in my purse.

James hadn't mentioned where we were going, and as part of my new life philosophy I hadn't asked.

"Aren't you curious where I'm taking you?" he said in that low voice of his.

"No, I trust you."

We were stopped at a red light. He turned to stare at me. "How do you know I'm trustworthy?"

"How do I know that you aren't?"

James abruptly pulled the car into another lane. "We're going to California, right this instant."

I didn't blink.

"If I drove you to the airport and told you to get on a plane to California, you'd follow me."

"Why not?"

"Unfortunately, I'm only taking you to dinner, Naomi. Maybe a movie. If I'd known it was your birthday, I would have planned something more exciting."

But just being with James was exciting. I liked that his past was as much a mystery as mine. I liked that he might do anything at any moment. I liked that he didn't expect me to behave any specific way. I liked that he believed me when I said I would take off and go to California.

"Maybe I'll have to take you to California sometime?"

"What's in California?"

"Kick-ass waves. I'm an amateur surfer and the Atlantic don't really cut it," he said. "My dad is, too. He lives in L.A."

"Are you from there?"

"The thing is, I'm not really from anywhere, you know what I mean?"

I did.

"But yeah, I lived there for a while. Until I came here to live with my mom and my grandfather, and . . . I'd like to go back there for school. To the film program at USC, if I get in."

On the way to the restaurant, it had started to snow.

By the time the movie was over, the town was a different place, the negative image of itself. I felt almost newborn myself, like it was my first winter ever.

"I wonder if there's enough snow on the steps at school for us to go sledding," James said.

We left his car at the movie theater and walked over to Tom Purdue, which was about a mile away. I was freezing, but I didn't care. I bet the weather was worse in Kratovo.

We trudged across the campus to the entrance of Tom Purdue. We stood at the bottom of the steps, which were entirely blanketed by snow.

"This is where we met," I pointed out.

"The lengths a girl will go to to meet a boy," he deadpanned. "We need sleds."

I told him I didn't know where we could find any.

"No, like cafeteria trays or garbage can lids or something. Unfortunately, school's closed."

Luckily, I had my yearbook keys. I ran inside and located two plastic lids right in the front hallway.

"Let's go," I said. I didn't bother to mention to James that I was supposed to be avoiding sports on account of my head. I didn't really care.

My first few times down the hill I couldn't really control the "sled," and I got sent down at strange angles.

James was better than me. He showed me how to position my body and back so that I was in the middle and leaning forward. My next attempts were better.

"Who needs the Pacific?" he yelled.

We sledded down the steps until eleven-thirty. It was like meeting him over and over again.

We sledded until I couldn't even make one more trip up the stairs. My cheeks were flushed, my lips were chapped, and every part of me was wet or sticky with snow. I was so cold, I was past feeling cold at all. I lay down in the snow at the bottom of the stairs. I felt like I was becoming an ice person and that when it became warm again, I would probably melt and disappear.

James kept sledding even after I had stopped. He went up and down five or six more times before parking himself at my feet. For the longest time he only looked at me.

"Lying there, you look like an angel," he said softly.

I didn't speak.

"Funny thing is, I don't believe in angels."

He offered me his hand, and we walked back to my house in the bright, early hours of Sunday.

He kissed me when we got to the door, and even though it was late, I invited him inside. Dad had gone out with Rosa Rivera, and for all I knew he was probably snowed in somewhere or other. James was shivering nearly as much as me at this point.

I brought him some clothes from Dad's closet and he changed into them. "I'll get my dad to drive you to your car when he gets back."

James nodded and sat down at our kitchen table.

"Seventeen," he said. "You're still a baby."

"Why? How old are you?"

"I'll be nineteen in February."

"That's not that old."

"Feels plenty old to me sometimes," he said. "I was held back a grade." He shrugged.

I smiled at him. "I've heard the rumors about you, you know?"

"Oh yeah, like what?"

I listed the most interesting ones: 1) he used drugs, 2) he went crazy over some girl at his old school, and 3) he had tried to kill himself and had been in a hospital.

James ran his fingers through his hair, which was still damp from the snow. "All true. Technically, the drugs were prescribed. And technically, I may have tried to kill myself *twice*, but basically all true. Does it matter?" His voice had changed. "Think. Think before you answer. It's allowed to matter."

I told him that it didn't.

"I would have told you, but it's not something I like to talk about when I first meet someone, or ever, and also . . ." His eyes were turned toward the window, but I could tell he was really watching me. "I wanted you to *like* me."

"Why?"

"You seemed like a person who it might be nice to be liked by. I haven't thought that about anybody for a while." I had thought the same thing about him.

I put my arm around him. Neither of us moved or spoke for the longest time. "I can leave now," he said, "and then we could just go on from there. Friends, maybe?"

I took his face in my hands and I told him none of it mattered to me at all.

That's when he told me everything. For a guy who said "screw the past," James certainly had a lot of it.

It had all started the year his brother died of lung cancer. James was fifteen. Sasha was eighteen, the same age James was now.

The night before Sasha's funeral, James swallowed an entire bottle of a prescription his brother had been taking. They thought James was trying to kill himself, but he hadn't been. He had just wanted something that would help him sleep through the night. In a weird way, James said it made him feel closer to Sasha, having his brother's pills inside.

James's mom found him, and he had his stomach pumped. They sent him to his first doctor, who gave James his first antidepressant. He was supposed to go to therapy, but he never went. The drugs screwed with his head, made him feel kind of numb, which James said was all right by him.

Things were good for a while, only insofar as they weren't too bad. By then James was sixteen, and he had met Sera. James said that they told each other they were in love, but looking back, he said they hadn't been. Puppy love, if anything, he said. He might have only said this so as not to hurt my feelings.

At some point, he realized that the drugs weren't working anymore. He started feeling jumpy all the time. Kids were looking at him funny; he was pretty sure they were talking about him, too. James cursed out one of his teachers. Sera broke up with him.

He stopped taking the pills to try to get Sera back, but she'd started going out with this other guy.

One night, he crawled into her bedroom window. She wasn't there. James said he was so lonely, he had just wanted to be with her things. He saw a packing knife on her desk, and it suddenly seemed like a really good idea to slit his wrists.

After that, things got hazy.

In the hospital, they said Sera's mom was the one who had found him. James still felt bad about this. Sera's mom was a nice lady, he said. Sera, too, for that matter. James saw now that none of it had been her fault.

James was sent to the East Coast, where his mom lived. He was in an institution for about six months, which was not something he liked to talk about. When he got out, his parents said James could go back to his old school in California, but he didn't see the point. James was eighteen by then, and had been held back a year, and anyone who remembered him at his old school thought he was crazy.

That's when James met me. That day, he'd only been there to drop off his old school records. He hadn't been planning or wanting to meet anyone. If he hadn't stopped for a smoke, he wouldn't have met me at all. He patted the pocket where he kept his smokes. "Always knew these would be the death of me." He smiled when he said this.

My phone rang. It was Dad; he said he was staying at Rosa Rivera's for the night on account of the snow.

"My dad can't get back tonight," I said to James.

"I should probably walk then. I don't want my mother to worry."

"Call her," I told him. "Let her know you're staying with friends."

"I don't lie," he said, shaking his head.

"Are you saying we're not friends?"

"I'm saying we're not just friends."

"Still, you can't go out in this."

"My mother worries," he repeated. It was like that day in Will's car when James hadn't wanted a ride even though it was pouring. He had a stubborn, tough, even masochistic streak, and he insisted that he leave then. All I could do was stand at the window and watch as he disappeared into that whitewashed night.

Seven

OF ALL THE STUPID THINGS TO BE FAILING, I WAS failing photography.

The last school day before Thanksgiving, Mr. Weir held me after class. I knew what he wanted to talk about. I still hadn't turned in a project proposal, and the semester was more than half over. Most of the classes were structured very loosely, with Mr. Weir showing slides of work by famous photographers like Doisneau or Mapplethorpe and us discussing them. The rest of the time we'd critique each other's work, though I hadn't brought in anything to critique all semester. Whenever Mr. Weir asked about my project (about once a week or so), I'd just B.S. something or other. The nature of the class made it easy to get away with doing nothing.

Mr. Weir handed me a slip. "I'm sorry to have to do this right before the holiday, Naomi," he said. "I've got to give this to anyone who is in danger of receiving a D or below. It requires a parent's signature."

"But, Mr. Weir, I thought our grade was based on the one big project."

"Yes, that's why I'm giving this to you now. You still have time to make it work."

James was waiting for me outside of Weir's class.

"Wondering if you need a ride?" he asked.

I had yearbook, of course.

"Do you have to?" James asked. "Everyone's gone for the holiday already."

Actually, there was tons of work to do in yearbook, not to mention that Will was pissed at me already. It had started just after my birthday.

"Did you get my mix?" he'd asked.

"Which one?"

"The one for your birthday."

"Yeah, but I haven't had time to listen to it yet."

"Well, that's rude," he'd said finally. "I spent a lot of time on that."

But what I had thought to myself at the time was: *How much time could he have possibly spent? The kid gives me a mix like every freaking week.*

Anyway, Will had been pretty icy to me since then, but I hadn't had time to deal with him.

"So," James was saying, "why don't I just take you out for coffee before you go to yearbook? I'll have you back by three-thirty, I swear."

James was wearing this black wool peacoat, which he looked particularly tall and handsome in. Some girls like suits or tuxedos;

I'm a sucker for a guy in a great coat. I knew I couldn't refuse him. Plus, after my talk with Mr. Weir, I really needed to get out of school.

We drove into town. James had a cup of black coffee and I had a glass of orange juice, and then we took our drinks outside and walked down the main strip of town. Even though the day was gray and moist, it was nice to be outside instead of where I was supposed to be: cooped up in that yearbook office where every part of me felt dried and tired, my hands always covered with these oppressive little paper cuts.

"I don't want to go back to yearbook," I said.

"So don't" was James's reply.

"I don't just mean today. I mean ever."

"So don't," he repeated.

"It's not that easy," I said. "People are counting on me."

"Honestly, Naomi, it's only a stupid high school yearbook. It's just a bunch of pictures and a cover. They make a million of them every year all around the world. I've been to three different high schools, and the yearbooks always look more or less the same. Trust me, the yearbook will get published with or without you. They'll find someone else to do your job."

I didn't reply. I was thinking how if I quit yearbook, I'd have more time for everything else: school, my photography class that I could no longer drop, therapy, and James, of course.

"It's three-thirty," James said after about ten minutes.

I told him I wanted to keep walking awhile, which we did. We didn't say much; above all, James was good at keeping quiet.

James dropped me off at school around five.

Since it was the night before the holiday, I knew most of the kids would be gone early. Except, of course, for Will.

From the beginning, the conversation did not go well. I tried to be nice. I tried to explain to Will about my schoolwork and my photography class. I tried to tell him how he could run the whole show without me, that he already had been anyway. Will wasn't hearing any of it, and before too long I found myself making some of James's points, which had made so much sense when I was outside in the daylight.

"It's just a stupid yearbook."

"*You* don't think that!"

"It's just a stack of photos in a binder!"

"No, this is all wrong."

"You said you'd understand if I had to quit!"

"I was being *polite*!" He was silent for a moment. "Is this because of James?"

I told him no, that I'd been unhappy for some time.

Will wouldn't look at me. "What is so great about him? Explain it to me."

"I don't have to justify myself to you, Will."

"I really want to know what is so f'n great about him. Because from my point of view, he looks like the moody guy on a soap opera."

"The *what*?"

"You heard me. With all his moping around and his brooding and his cigarettes and his cool haircut. What does he have to be so upset about?"

"For your information, not that it's any of your business, he has someone in his family who died."

"I was there when he said it, remember! And hey, let's throw a goddamn parade for James. Lots of people have people in their families who died, Naomi. I'd wager everybody in the whole damn world has people in their families who've died. But not all of us can afford to go around screwing things up all the time. Not all of us have the luxury of being so exquisitely depressed."

"You're being a jerk. I don't see why you're attacking James just because I don't want to be on yearbook!"

"Do you actually think you're in love with him?" Will laughed. " 'Cause if you do, I think you lost more than your memory in that fall."

"What are you saying?"

"I'm saying that you're acting like a dope. The Naomi I knew honors her commitments."

"Get it through your head. I'm not her anymore. I'm not the Naomi that you knew."

"No shit!" he yelled. "The Naomi I knew wasn't a selfish bitch."

"I hate you," I said.

"Good . . . I li-li-lia . . . Good!"

I started to leave.

"No, wait—"

I turned around.

"If you're really quitting, you need to give me your office keys."

"Right now?"

"I want to make sure you don't steal anything."

I took them out of my backpack and threw them in his face.

Sometimes these things take on a momentum of their own. I had gone in there just to quit yearbook, but I had ended up quitting

Will, too. Maybe it had been naive to think it could have gone any other way.

When I got outside, James was waiting for me.

"Thought you might need a ride," he said.

"But not home. Somewhere I haven't been before."

He drove me to the Sleepy Hollow Cemetery, which seemed a strange place to take a girl, but I went with it.

"There's a particular grave I want you to see," he said.

"You've been here already?"

James nodded. "I've been to a lot of cemeteries. Sera and I went to Jim Morrison's grave in Paris and we saw Oscar Wilde's at Père-Lachaise, too. Wilde's was covered in lipstick prints."

I asked him how he'd gotten into visiting graveyards.

"Well . . . when my brother died, I guess. I liked thinking of all the others who had also died. It seemed less lonely somehow. Knowing that there are more of them than us, Naomi."

He took me to the grave of Washington Irving, who wrote the novella *The Legend of Sleepy Hollow*. I don't know what kind of rock the headstone was made from, but at this point it was white from time. The stone was so worn away you could barely make out the inscription. It was a simple tombstone, just his name and dates.

"Most famous people tend to go that way, no epitaphs," James said. "That's what I'd do."

"You've thought about it?"

"Oh, only a little," he said with a wry grin.

It was pleasant in the graveyard. Silent. Empty and yet not empty. It was a good place for forgetting things. My phone rang. It was Will. I turned it off.

"That story reminds me of you," he said.

I didn't necessarily take that as a compliment. We had read *Sleepy Hollow* in Mrs. Landsman's class around Halloween. It was something of a tradition in Tarrytown, where the book is set. (Technically, North Tarrytown, where James lived, was the true Sleepy Hollow.) It was about "the ghost of a Hessian trooper whose head had been carried away by a cannon-ball, in some nameless battle during the revolutionary war" and who was said to "[ride] forth to the scene of battle in nightly quest of his head."

"You think of me as a headless horseman?" I asked.

"I think of you as a person on a quest," James said.

"What does that mean?"

He was standing behind me, and he put his arms around me. "I think of you as someone who is figuring things out under difficult circumstances. Despite the fact that I am falling in love with you, I think that I am likely to be a brief chapter in this quest. I want you to keep sight of that."

He had never said "love" before, and I suppose it should have thrilled me. The fact that the "love" was in a clause took a bit away from the moment, though. I asked him what he was really saying.

"I want you to know that I don't expect anything from you." James took my hand and turned me around, so that we were looking eye to eye. "I need to take pills to keep me steady," he said, "but you make me feel the opposite. I worry about that. I worry for you. That's why I fought this. You. Us. I'm not even sure I trust myself with anybody now, but . . .

"If things start to go bad . . . I mean, if I start to go bad, I want you to break up with me. I won't fight you on it. I promise."

"What if I fight you? Aren't I allowed to do that?" I asked.

He shook his head. "Promise me you won't, though."

"I can't do that."

"You have to, otherwise we can't be together. I swear to God, I'll end it right now. If I get sick again, I don't want you to come visit me or even think about me. I want you to forget we ever met. Forget me."

I knew that would be impossible, but I crossed my fingers and told him I would.

I spent Thanksgiving alone with Dad. Rosa Rivera had gone to Boston to spend the day with her two daughters. James went to L.A. to see his father.

My dad cooked way too much too-rich food; we ate nearly nothing, and then Dad drove the rest over to a local food bank.

My mother called my cell phone in the afternoon while Dad was out. I had been ignoring her thrice-weekly messages since September, but I was feeling pretty blue that Thanksgiving so I picked up.

"Hi," I said.

"Nomi," she said, shocked at getting me. "I was just going to leave a message."

"I can hang up and then you can still do that."

Mom didn't say anything for a moment. "How are you?"

"I'm good," I said.

"Did you get the coat I sent you for your birthday?"

"I'm wearing it right now." It was red with tortoiseshell buttons and a hood. I felt like Little Red Riding Hood in it, but it was warm.

"Your dad likes the house pretty frigid."

"He's getting better. It's not his fault; it's me. I'm always cold."

"I know. Dad told me."

"I should go. I have some schoolwork to do."

"Okay. I love you, Nomi."

"I should go."

"Okay. Oh wait, I actually had a reason for calling . . ."

"Yeah?"

"Dad said you were having some trouble in photography. I could help. I do that, you know."

"It's not trouble. I just have to turn in this assignment. I . . . I really have to go."

"Thanks for picking up," she said.

We said goodbye and I hung up the phone. I didn't want her goddamn help. She was always trying to find ways to insinuate herself back into my life.

And yet, I wondered . . .

If I had forgiven Dad for lying to me about Rosa Rivera, why couldn't I seem to do even half that for Mom?

When it came down to it, I didn't even know why I was in a fight with Mom. I knew the reasons, yes, but the fight itself was just a story I had been told.

I was thinking about calling Mom again when Dad came home.

He turned on the television and started watching a program about the meerkat. "The meerkat," said the narrator, "is one of the few mammals other than humans to teach their young. Watch the adult parent show its child how to remove the venomous stinger from the scorpion before eating it."

"Sweet, right?" Dad said.

"What are you planning to teach me?" I asked Dad.

An ad came on and Dad pressed mute on the television. "Unfortunately, your old man is pretty unskilled. I know a bit about cooking and travel. And a very little bit about writing and animals, but other than that, you'd be better off with a meerkat for a pop, I suspect."

We watched three more nature programs in a row—one on pandas (cute to look at, but basically jerks), one on eagles, and another on bobcats. The one we were currently watching was called *Top Ten Smelliest Animals*, which was pretty much Dad's ideal program, combining list-making and nature as it were.

During another ad I asked Dad, "Is this how you spent a lot of time before you met Rosa Rivera?"

He pressed mute again. "Yeah, I was pretty bad there for a while," he admitted.

I considered this.

"What's Mom's husband like?"

Dad nodded and then nodded some more. "He's in building restoration. Nice guy, I think. Nice-looking. There're probably better people to sing his praises than me."

"And Chloe?"

"Smart, she says, but then you were, too. Cass and I, we pretty much thought you were the best little kid in the world, you know? We always said it was a good piece of luck, you getting left in that typewriter case."

I nodded.

"Will coming by today?" Dad asked.

I shook my head. I hadn't told Dad about quitting yearbook or our fight.

"You're not spending as much time with him these days," Dad said.

"I think we're growing apart," I said.

"Happens," Dad said. "He's a good egg, though. Takes care of his mom since his father died. Hard worker. Always been a good friend to you."

"Will's father died?" I asked. He had never mentioned it.

"Yes, that's why they moved to Tarrytown. His mother wanted a good school where she could get free tuition for Will by teaching."

I nodded.

The program came on again and Dad turned up the volume.

Since it was Thanksgiving, I thought about calling Will on the phone and making up with him, but I couldn't bring myself to do it. Our fight didn't even have a scab yet, and in my mind he'd said worse things to me than I had to him.

When James got back on Saturday afternoon, he said he had an idea for my photography project. At his dad's in California, James had noticed all these old cameras. He asked his dad if he could have them, and his dad said sure, because what else was there to do with a bunch of old cameras anyway. They were a pain really—you didn't want to throw them out because of their perceived value, so they basically ended up taking up space.

"So, it's supposed to be a personal story, right?" James asked. "My idea is that we go back to those steps at Tom Purdue with my dad's old cameras and throw them down the steps, simulating your own journey two and a half months ago. In theory, the camera will take the picture either en route or at the point of impact. It'll be an exercise in point of view. Does that sound like something Weir would like?"

"Sounds perfect."

"We're gonna need more cameras, though," James said.

On Sunday morning we went in search of cheap cameras to throw down the stairs. The first place we went was the local pharmacy, where we bought five disposable cameras of various makes for around ten bucks apiece and fifteen rolls of film. James tried to pay, but I wouldn't let him. It was my project after all.

We also went to a vintage electronics and repair store in downtown Tarrytown where we found four cameras in a dusty metal trash bin for five bucks apiece. We hoped they would still be functional, but we wouldn't know until we saw the film.

The owner of the store kept looking at me strangely as I was paying. James had gone outside for a smoke.

"The record player," he said finally. "You never came for it."

"What record player?"

"You paid to get one fixed around the beginning of August, but you never came to pick it up."

The owner ran into the back room and came out with a record player. The base was cherry with a pattern of swirls carved into the side. It was pretty, I guess, though I couldn't imagine why I'd been getting one repaired. I didn't have a single record.

My name was taped to the front: NAOMI PORTER.

Clearly, it was mine. I wondered what it was for.

"Use it in good health," said the storekeeper.

When I got outside, James looked at me curiously. "Impulse buy?" he asked as he helped me put the record player in the backseat of his car.

We spent the rest of the afternoon throwing cameras down the steps of Tom Purdue. Some of them had timers, which we could set prior to throwing them. With others, we'd press the button and throw the camera really fast to get the shot in midair. Still others were total Hail Marys and we hoped they'd land on the button and take a picture as they hit the ground. I had no idea what sort of images we were getting, but at least it was fun.

On the second-to-last camera, James cut his thumb on one of the shattered lenses. He didn't even realize it until I pointed it out to him. "How could you not notice?" I asked him.

James laughed. "I'm used to bleeding for you." He held up his palm. I kissed it, right in the middle. I was about to move from palm to mouth when I saw Will watching us from the front doors of the school. When he caught my eye, he came outside really fast and started heading down the stairs.

"Hello, Naomi," he said. "Larkin."

"Hi," I said.

"Working on the weekend?" James asked Will.

"Never stops," Will said stiffly. "You're bleeding, Larkin."

"I blame her," James said.

"Naomi," Will said softly, "do you really think you should be running up and down these stairs without a helmet?"

"A *what*?" James asked.

"You know, for her head. If she reinjured herself—"

I cut him off. "I'm fine, Will."

Will just nodded. "See you around. Naomi. James." He nodded again as he said each of our names and then he was gone.

"It's lucky he didn't see us sledding." James touched my forehead. "You'd look pretty cute in a helmet actually."

Because he was cut, I tried to send James home without me, but he wouldn't go. He insisted on helping me pick up the camera carcasses, which I was against. "When I was a kid," he said, "I had a tendency to let other people clean up my messes. I'm trying not to be that way anymore."

I pointed out that this wasn't his mess; it was mine.

"Still," said James. By then, the blood was practically pouring from his thumb. I wondered if he needed stitches.

"You wouldn't be abandoning me if you stopped to get a Band-Aid, you know."

I didn't have time to develop the film in the school's lab until the following Wednesday.

There wasn't much to look at. A few shots of sky. Some concrete. A lot of black. Still, the point wasn't always that the pictures be pretty, was it? Sometimes it was about the process, like with Jackson Pollock paintings. As I made enlargements of the photos, I hoped that Mr. Weir would see it that way.

Mr. Weir hated my project. "It's an interesting gimmick, but it wasn't the assignment. Your assignment was to tell a personal story in pictures."

"This is a personal story." I defended my project. "This is exactly what happened to me."

"Naomi, don't misunderstand me. I'm not saying that this isn't personal. It's simply that the assignment counts for your whole grade, and I'm expecting something deeper."

When the bell rang, I took my pictures with me and stuffed them in my locker.

"What did Weir think?" James asked. He was standing behind me at my locker.

"He didn't get it."

Blank-slate time all over again.

Saturday afternoon, James, Alice, Yvette, and I took the train into the city to see a show. We hadn't decided what we would see, and when we got there most everything was sold out. There were a couple of tickets left for the Rockettes' Holiday Spectacular at Radio City Music Hall, so we went to that, despite the fact that Alice found it "degrading to women" and James found it "campy."

Even if you have no interest in lines of aging showgirls wearing too much makeup kicking up their legs, there's something impressive about it. Something *spectacular*. It's like a sicko cloning experiment.

At intermission, James went outside for a smoke, and I went to the bathroom. Alice and Yvette remained in the theater to argue about whether the show was "objectifying women" (Alice) or "celebrating their athleticism" (Yvette). I didn't necessarily think the two positions were irresolvable.

There was a long line outside the bathroom. I wondered if I would make it through before the show started again. Not that it mattered. The spectacular didn't have a story you had to follow—it was just a bunch of women standing in a row.

Someone placed a hand on my shoulder.

"Naomi Porter?"

I turned around. It was a Japanese guy, maybe in his thirties. He was wearing expensive black glasses, a Rolling Stones T-shirt, a red hoodie, charcoal pin-striped pants, and black Converse sneakers. He was holding the hand of a little girl in a gray dress with hearts on it and pink sneakers, Converses like her dad's.

"You probably don't remember me," he said. "I'm Nigel Fusakawa."

The name was familiar.

"Cass's husband," he added. "Everyone calls me Fuse."

He stuck out his hand, and without thinking I shook it.

"She was supposed to come today, but she has a bit of a cold."

I nodded.

"Could you do me a favor?" he asked. "I'm here by myself. Would you mind taking Chloe to the bathroom?"

"I—"

"It would really help us out."

I looked at the little girl. She was sweet, shyer in person than she had been on the phone. Besides, none of what had happened was her fault. I nodded toward Fuse. We were about to enter the interior part of the bathroom, and I took Chloe's hand.

"What's your name?" she squeaked.

"I'm Nomi," I said.

Her eyes grew very wide. "Nobody?"

"Sure, whatever."

I let her go first. "Do you need any help?"

"No, I've been doing this myself forever," she informed me. I wondered how long forever was. A year? Six months? "I could have gone in here myself, but my daddy doesn't want me to get raped."

"Raped?" I nearly burst out laughing. Did she even know what that meant?

"That happens all the time in bathrooms," she informed me seriously.

She had Mom's blue eyes and Fuse's black hair. She was cute. She remembered to wash her hands without my prompting.

"Daddy says you're my sister," she said as we were on the way out.

What was I going to do? Tell her it wasn't true? "Yeah," I said.

"I don't want to be anyone's sister," she said.

"Why not?"

"Because I want to be the only one."

"You'll still be the only one," I said.

She pursed her tiny rosebud mouth. She didn't look at all convinced.

Fuse was waiting for us right outside the door. "Thanks for saving me from having to be the only man in the women's room."

"Don't mention it."

"Naomi," Fuse asked, "I hope this isn't too forward, but why don't you come over to our apartment after the show? We live about twenty blocks up from here, and I know Cass would be so, so, so psyched to see you. Chloe and I would be glad to have you, too."

"I'm . . . I can't . . . I'm with friends," I said.

"Bring them along. Really. Please. Cass would kill me if I didn't try to get you up to our house. She's really missed you. I know, trust me I know, things have been hard between you, but it's nearly

175

Christmas, and what luck us running into you, and isn't that the coat she sent you for your birthday?"

I nodded. This guy knew so much about me without my knowing a thing about him.

"I helped her pick it out. She'd be really glad to see you in it. Did you get the pictures from your friend?"

I had no idea what he was talking about. "What pictures?"

"Nothing. I . . . I must have gotten confused. We'll meet you right here by the bathroom, okay? The Radio City Music Hall ladies' room. It's our special place," he said with a wink.

The guy sounded sort of desperate, and the little girl was staring at me. The whole situation was starting to get incredibly awkward. A light flashed indicating that intermission was over.

"Please come. I know you weren't planning to run into us; I know this isn't how you were thinking you would spend your day. But now we have and it's lucky, I think. Please, Naomi."

He was begging. I didn't want the little girl to have to watch her father beg, so I found myself saying yes.

During the second half of the show, the kicking had lost its novelty for me and the women's identical painted-on smiles were giving me a headache. It occurred to me that if any of the Rockettes got sick or even murdered, no one would notice. They'd just bring on an identical replacement, smack on some lipstick, and the show would go on without any noticeable decrease in quality. Somewhere, some poor Rockette would be dead and buried, and the only people who would notice or care at all would be her family. The thought made me depressed as anything.

I whispered to James that I needed to leave, and he told Alice and Yvette. "It's her head," he said. It was my built-in, all-purpose excuse.

"Do you want us to come with you, cookie?" Alice whispered sympathetically.

"No, watch the rest of the show," I whispered back. "We'll take the train back early."

I didn't tell James about running into Fuse and Chloe. When we got outside I said, "I couldn't be in there anymore, you know?"

"Sure," he said.

"I don't feel like going back yet, though." I was too wound up from running into my mother's new family.

James didn't ask me why, only what I wanted to do instead. I couldn't think of anything—most of the things I knew were in Brooklyn—so I told him that we should just ride the subways for a while.

We rode all the way down to the South Ferry stop and then all the way up to Van Cortlandt Park and then back to Grand Central. It took three hours total.

We didn't really talk much during that time. We watched people get off and on the train. There were lots of shopping bags owing to the time of year, and the people carrying them all seemed tired to me, but warily optimistic. It put me in mind of Fuse asking me over to Mom's house. I wondered how long he and Chloe had waited by the restroom at Radio City Music Hall.

"I have this sister . . ." I said to James right before we were about to get off the subway.

"You never said."

"Well, she's not technically related to me, so . . ." All of a sudden, it seemed too difficult to explain. Where would I start? From the typewriter case in Moscow Oblast? It would be a very long story. "She's almost four," I said. "Roughly the same number of years I lost, you know? Like, if you could take all that time and make a person, it would be her."

"But you can't do that." James shook his head. "My brother," he began before shaking his head again. "I don't want to talk about this."

"Please, say it."

"Sasha lived eighteen years on this earth, and all that time didn't add up to a damn thing. What that time is to me now, is a hole. I . . . I wish he'd never been born or that I'd never been born. I can't talk about this."

He kissed me then and I suppose I was glad for the distraction.

By the time we had gotten on the Metro North Railroad back to Tarrytown, it was pretty late. Having gotten a ride from Alice that morning, we had to call James's mom, Raina, to pick us up at the train station.

Raina smelled like cigarettes and perfume, and she had this way of looking like she hadn't seen James in years. "Is everything okay? What happened to the friend who drove you? I didn't know you were going to be so late," she said. "I thought the play was a matinee." Even though she looked on the young side, she was all mom when it came to James.

"It's fine, Ma. It's . . . nothing," James said. "Ma, this is my friend, Naomi. You remember her? She was in that play I worked on."

She appraised me, and then we shook hands.

"Raina," she said.

"Nice to meet you."

She nodded. "I like your hair."

Raina dropped me off at my house first. James walked me to my door.

"Sorry about my mom," he said. "She's really protective."

I said something about that just being the way parents were.

"No, it's not like that," James said. "Raina's protective because I've given her reason to be. I've spent most of my teen years a complete and utter disaster. She's already lost so much. I guess she's always on the lookout for signs that I might turn bad again." His voice made a strange tremor over the word *bad*, and it made me want to kiss him, so I did.

I loved kissing him. I loved the way his mouth felt on mine. His lips were supple, but always a little chapped. The cigarettes (and the peppermints he ate to cover them up) made him taste bittersweet. But I wondered if all this kissing was a bad habit with him and me. The thing we did with our mouths instead of talking.

The time between Thanksgiving and Christmas always passes in about a minute. Before I knew it, James was leaving for Los Angeles to visit his father again, and Dad and I went to Pleasantville to spend the holidays with Rosa Rivera and her twin daughters, Frida and Georgia (aka Freddie and George), who she referred to as "the girls."

Although they were identical twins, Freddie and George did not look at all alike. George competed on her university's bodybuilding team, and she was packed with muscles. Freddie was petite, like

Rosa. Neither was shy about asking a lot of questions, as I would find out seated between them at dinner.

"Mom said you lost your memory?" George began.

I nodded.

"Our dad had Alzheimer's, did Mom say?" Freddie asked.

"I heard," I said. "I'm sorry."

"It sucked," George said. "It turned him into a total asshole."

"George!" Rosa Rivera yelled across the table.

"What? It did."

"But that's not what she has," Freddie said. "Mom said she only forgot the last four years?"

"Well, those years suck anyway," Freddie said. "Do you remember, George?"

"Man, we had those, like, mullets in seventh grade. What was Mom thinking?"

Freddie shook her head. "Do you have any idea what it's like to be known as the mullet twins?"

"I wish I could forget it," George said.

I laughed. "By the way, have we met before?" I asked.

"Yeah, we didn't really like you."

"We pretty much thought you were a typical snotty teenager."

"Kind of a jerk."

"Georgia and Frida Rivera!" Rosa Rivera yelled across the table. "That is not polite."

"What? We did. She's not offended."

I wasn't. I appreciated their honesty.

"You seem okay now, though."

For Christmas, Rosa Rivera gave me a pair of fur-lined gloves, and my dad gave me a memoir about climbing Everest. My mother sent me things to help with my photography class: monographs by Cindy Sherman, Rineke Dijkstra, and Diane Arbus, and a new camera, which I left in the box. It was lucky my project with James had already turned into a bust, otherwise that shiny new camera might have found itself taking a trip down the stairs. James bought me two goldfish in a heart-shaped glass bowl with a castle in it. We named them Sid and Nancy. They both died before break was over.

Eight

I WAS IN JAMES'S ROOM, LYING NEXT TO HIM IN bed. At Tom Purdue, there's a one-week reading period during January before exams where classes don't meet and you just review. I was studying physics; James was studying me. "I don't like to feel so crazy about someone," he said. "I don't like to feel like my happiness is so tied up in another person."

I said not to worry.

James sat up in bed and said, "No, I'm serious. Today, I almost forgot to take my pill. The way I feel about you . . . sometimes it scares me."

I started kissing him all over. Not just on the mouth—in my opinion, the mouth gets too much attention. There are a million equally interesting and lovely spaces to put lips to. I kissed him on the crease behind his knee. I kissed him on the small of his back, which was narrow but surprisingly muscular. I kissed him on the round bone that stuck out from the ankle; I don't know what that's called. I kissed him on his eyebrows, which were dark and well forested and just a hair or two shy of a unibrow. I kissed him on his wrist, right on top of that two-inch horizontal scar.

He pulled his wrist away from me.

"Don't," I said.

He laughed. "God, I was so stupid back then."

"Do you mean for trying to kill yourself?"

He laughed a little longer, and a little more sadly somehow. "No. I just meant that if you're slitting your wrists, you're supposed to do it vertically, not horizontally. If you cut horizontally, you don't bleed enough. The wound begins to heal on its own."

My worst subject, aside from photography, was French. I had to study like a fiend just to pass, and even then I didn't know as many vocabulary words as required for the most elementary conversations.

As luck would have it, James was a whiz at French. The private school he had gone to in California started teaching the subject nearly simultaneously with English. He would sometimes help me study by having conversations with me *en français* where he would introduce new words that I hadn't yet covered.

We were in his car when he asked me, in French, "Do you blame Will Landsman or the stairs for your accident?"

I had to ask him to translate, because stairs was outside of my limited vocabulary. Accident, however, was not.

Once he'd translated, I replied without really thinking, *"Ni l'un ni l'autre. L'appareil-photo,"* meaning "Neither, I blame the camera."

James laughed. "Hey, that was good."

The strange thing was I hadn't known I knew the words for "neither" or "camera" until I said them.

We were driving to his job at the community college (he was doing American Cinema that semester), and I remember looking at the trees and knowing that they were *arbres*.

That the road was *route*.

And the sky, *ciel*.

And marble.

And coin toss.

And coffee cup.

And the French words for everything under the sun.

I was about to tell James that my French had, unexpectedly, seemed to return, when I realized that it was not alone.

I remembered everything.

Everything *everything*.

Starting with that day.

Will and I had been arguing about who should have to go back to the office to get the camera.

Will removed a quarter from his pocket, and without even asking he announced that I would be tails and he, heads.

So I joked, "Who made you God?"

"Naomi," he asked, "are you saying you'd prefer to be heads?"

I wasn't necessarily saying that—I didn't really care either way—but my friend (and co-editor) could be efficient to the point of dictatorial, and as his co-editor (and friend), I thought that this was something he needed to work on. "People appreciate being asked," I said. "As a courtesy, you know?"

Will sighed. "Heads or tails?"

I called heads just as he threw the coin. It was, in some respects, a decent throw—high enough that I momentarily lost track of it, though this might have been an illusion caused by the silver against the twilight. High enough that I wondered if Will, who was not known for his athletic prowess, would actually manage to catch it. He didn't. The coin landed with an undignified plop in a puddle seven feet over, on the border between the student and faculty parking lots. We raced over to verify the results. I was fast from tennis and I got there first. Through the murky water I could make out the hazy outline of an eagle.

"Should have stuck with tails, Chief," he said, fishing George Washington out of the puddle.

"Yeah, yeah."

We parted by shaking hands, which was how my colleague and I always said goodbye.

I trudged across the faculty parking lot and across the school's two athletic fields—our paltry marching band (twenty-three members) was practicing on one, and our paltry football team (average height: five feet eight inches) on the other.

I trudged up the hill that began at the lower-school (grades 7–9) buildings and peaked at the upper school (10–12) in an impressive display of topographical symbolism.

I trudged up the twenty-five marble steps that led to the entrance of the main building; the brick, banklike structure people thought of when they thought of Tom Purdue, largely because it was on the cover of all the brochures. At this point, it was nearly seven o'clock and the halls were empty, the way you'd expect them to be at nearly seven o'clock. I unlocked the door to *The Phoenix*—no one was there since school hadn't even started—and retrieved the camera, which was new enough that we hadn't even had time to buy a carrying case or a strap yet.

In the time all this took, it had officially become dark, and I was ready to be home. I jogged out of the building and down the marble stairs.

People said I had tripped—as in *Did-you-hear-what-happened-to-Naomi-Porter-she-tripped-going-down-the-stairs-and-her-brain-exploded*—but that wasn't what happened.

Think about it. I was not an eighty-year-old woman with a creaky hip, and at that point I had been climbing those Tom Purdue steps for almost four years: seventh, eighth, ninth, and tenth grades. I knew how they felt when they were slick with rain. I knew how they felt when wearing heels and a formal dress. I knew how they felt in the middle of winter, coated with salt.

Those steps could not have been more familiar to me, so that's why it was impossible that I could have *tripped*.

What really happened was that someone had left a Styrofoam coffee cup on the steps. In the darkness I didn't see it, so I kicked the cup and whatever was inside spilled out. I remember slipping a bit on the liquid and that's when I lost my grip on the camera. In that split second before diving down the stairs, my only thoughts were for the camera, and how it had cost *The Phoenix* a heck of a lot of money, and how much I wanted to catch it before it hit the stairs.

I didn't trip or fall—tripping and falling are accidents.

I dove—diving is intentional. Idiotic, yes, but also intentional.

Diving is a leap of faith plus gravity.

I had been throwing myself toward something.

Maybe away from something else.

I had kissed Will the night before.

Actually, he had kissed me, but I hadn't stopped it.

It had happened quickly; we were covering the Science Club's back-to-school trip to the planetarium. I had always teased Will about his obsessive coverage of academia. Will's "Nerd Inclusion Campaign" I called it, even though that was probably mean, and let's face facts, we were both kind of nerds ourselves. In any case, we decided to stay for the star show.

So we kissed. I think we had both been tricked by the air-conditioning and the darkness and all those treacherous fake stars.

That kiss had probably been more about my ambivalence toward Ace than any romantic notions I had had about Will. Besides, I hadn't met James yet.

In all these months, Will had never mentioned it, though. I suppose it didn't matter anyhow. I was with James now, and Will and I weren't even friends.

Sitting in James's car, I took off my sunglasses even though we were in the midst of a brilliant, white January sunset.

We were stopped at a traffic light when James said to me, "You're awfully quiet."

I nodded blankly and tried to smile. I felt like if I spoke, I might have an aneurysm.

"You aren't wearing your sunglasses," he said.

"Oh . . ." I put them back on. Then I kissed James on the mouth, probably too hard.

I decided that I wouldn't tell him or anyone else about my remembering. In a way, none of it mattered. None of it changed anything.

This was what I told myself.

I looked at James. I looked at him and felt grateful again that he'd been the one at the bottom of the stairs. It could have been anyone.

For obvious reasons, my exams went much better than expected, my French exam particularly. I did so well that Mrs. Greenberg decided to base my grade solely on the final. She was a tough teacher, but always, always fair. "You have had much to deal with, Naomi," she said in French, "but you have studied hard and come out beautifully."

I understood her perfectly and expressed my gratitude in French.

At his request, I went to see Mr. Weir on the last day of finals. "Congratulations. You have eighteen more weeks to dazzle me," he said. Instead of failing me, he was giving me an incomplete. Incidentally, if I'd had my memory back in September, I definitely would have dropped that class. His was the worst kind of elective—the kind with the potential to bring down your GPA.

When I got back home that night, Dad was in his study working.

I quietly took the car keys off the hook by the kitchen door and went for a drive.

It felt good to be behind the wheel again.

I didn't drive anywhere in particular. I stayed in my neighborhood, making enough right turns so that I ended up back where I started.

When I was about seven years old, I got lost in a museum. My parents had been researching their third or fourth Wandering Porters book, the one in the South of France. I had thought I was with my mother, but I hadn't been. I had been mistakenly following a woman with a camera bag that looked like hers. When the woman turned, I realized my error and began to cry.

The woman looked at me and although she did not speak English (I don't think she was French either), I managed to detect the question ". . . *Maman . . . ?*"

I nodded miserably and pointed to the camera.

"*L'appareil-photo?*"

I nodded even more miserably. As it happened, my mother entered the gallery then, and I was found.

For many years, *l'appareil-photo* was the only French word I had.

I don't know why my memory came back that day in James's car—maybe there was some medical explanation having to do with synapses and neurons—just as I don't know for certain why it left in the first place.

All I knew was that I missed my mother.

Nine

I DIDN'T WANT TO TELL ANYONE ABOUT THE END OF my amnesia, and the effort of keeping track of what I was and wasn't supposed to remember was exhausting me to where I began to forget insignificant things. Like my history book. The first day of the new semester, I lost mine. I thought it might have been in James's car— we had passed many enjoyable hours in there. I walked over to James's house to see if I could look around.

James was at work, so the car wasn't even there. I asked Raina if I could go look in his room, and she said to "be her guest." Raina had not been particularly warm, but James said it wasn't about me and I shouldn't take offense.

I looked under James's bed. Improbable as it may seem, my book was there: the mythic first place I had looked. As I was taking it out, my eyes alighted on something else.

It was a still-sealed envelope from the University of Southern

California, where James had applied early. It was postmarked December 13. James had left it unopened for seven weeks. It seemed a little, for lack of a better word, crazy. I mean, I knew that he had really wanted to go to the film program there, but was he so afraid of not being accepted that he wouldn't even open the envelope?

The right thing would have been to leave it there, but I didn't do that. I picked it up and put it in my pocket. I wasn't sure what I was going to do with it, but I couldn't bear the thought of it lying there under his bed.

He called me after work that night. He said that Raina had mentioned my visit and that he was sorry he'd missed me.

I told him that I'd been looking for my book when I'd accidentally stumbled upon the letter.

James grew deathly quiet.

"I could open it if you want," I said.

He didn't say anything.

"Are you that afraid of not getting in?"

He told me to mind my own goddamn business, and then he hung up on me. You could say that that was our first fight. He had never even raised his voice to me before. I suppose he was right to yell at me.

At school the next day, I didn't see him until lunch. I handed him the still-unopened letter and apologized if I had violated his privacy.

James took the letter. Without a word, he opened it. It was an acceptance. He set it on the ground, as if he couldn't care less. It started to blow away, so I put my boot heel on it.

"It's great news," I said. "It's what you wanted." I hugged him, but his posture was rigid. "What is it, Jims?"—that was my nickname for him—"Why aren't you happier?"

James explained, in an odd, low voice, "I hadn't been afraid that I wouldn't be accepted. I'd been afraid that I would."

I deluded myself into thinking he was talking about me—how we'd just met and now we'd be on two separate coasts or something like that.

By the time lunch ended, the coolness between us hadn't quite thawed.

After school, I was taking books from my locker when Ace Zuckerman came up to me. I hadn't spoken to him for months other than an occasional nod in the hallway. As I was still preoccupied with James and the whole acceptance business, I wasn't in the mood to talk to him now either.

Ace was captain of the tennis team that year, and he wanted to know if I was going to go out for it.

I said that I hadn't planned on it.

Ace was outraged. In addition to hair, the guy was incredibly passionate about tennis. "Well, you're a great player, and it would be a real shame for you not to play because of me."

"You?" I laughed. "Don't flatter yourself. I just don't want to play tennis anymore."

"You *love* tennis, Naomi. How can you not remember that?" Ace was standing really close to my face when, suddenly, something pulled him away. It was James, his eyes wild and blazing.

"Get the hell off of her!"

I tried to tell James that Ace and I had only been discussing tennis, but it was too late. These things tend to take on a momentum of their own.

Although James was wiry, he was not weak. He pulled Ace off of me and threw him against a locker. He punched him.

Ace hit him back, but mainly just to get James to stop attacking him. "You tool," Ace said. "We were only talking about tennis."

As I was trying to pull James off of Ace, James accidentally elbowed me in the eye. I knew without even seeing it that there was going to be a bruise.

Out of nowhere, Will Landsman got between Ace and James. I didn't even know he was in the hallway. "Everybody calm down," Will yelled. "You've just elbowed Naomi, you jerks!" Will shoved James with both his palms.

At this point, the assistant headmaster came out of her office to break it up.

James got a five-day suspension, and Ace, because he hadn't started it, three. Will and I both got one day of detention each, even though we'd only been bystanders. When I got home, my dad was pissed. He worried that my head couldn't take any more trauma.

"Who started it?" Dad demanded.

"I don't know." Of course it had been James, but I didn't want to tell him that. I repeated what I had thought at the time, "These things take on a momentum of their own."

Will and I served our detention together the next afternoon. We had to go pick up trash around the football field.

"This sucks. I was trying to break it up. I shouldn't even *be* here," he said.

"Who asked you to get involved? I was handling it."

"Nice shiner," Will muttered. "I have a million things to do. I've got to lock all the club pages. I have to decide who I'm sending to Philadelphia for Nationals. And, as you know, we are understaffed."

"We all have things to do," I said.

"What do you have? A packed schedule of hanging out with your exquisitely moody boyfriend?"

I didn't say anything. He was trying to pick a fight.

When I'd first heard about our detention, I had been thinking about taking the opportunity to make up with him. I had even been thinking about giving him that record player. When I got my memory back, I had remembered it was for him. Will had this huge collection of albums that he had inherited from his dad, only he never played them. He kept them hung on the wall, like posters. He'd never even had a record player. In any case, I had originally intended it as an "editor-to-editor, back-to-school" gift.

Looking at him, I could tell that too much had happened. We were past apologies and record players.

We didn't speak for the rest of the afternoon.

James's birthday was the Saturday before Valentine's Day. He hadn't told me—he was not big on birthdays—but I had seen it on his college forms.

I wanted to do something really nice for him because he seemed a little down.

I got Dad's permission to take him to the Hyde Park Drive-in in Poughkeepsie, which is about a seventy-minute drive from Tarrytown. They were having an Alfred Hitchcock festival, and James was such a movie buff.

It was a great day; the weather was really warm for February. We stayed to see two Hitchcock movies, *Vertigo* and *Psycho* ("Are you trying to tell me something?" James joked). Afterward we had dinner at a Friendly's, and everything was great until on the way home when James's car ran out of gas.

Honestly, I didn't think it was that big of a deal.

"We'll just call your mother," I said.

"I can't. I can't. She's already thinking I'm unstable because of the fight and the weirdness around the college letter. I can't give her one more thing. I can't." He was panicking.

"I'll call my dad." Unfortunately, Dad wasn't home and his cell phone was off. Even before I dialed, I remembered that he was at one of Rosa Rivera's tango exhibitions. Then I called Alice. She wasn't picking up either.

James finally agreed to phone his mother, who wasn't home anyway.

My dad got home around one a.m. and agreed to meet us with the fuel. We weren't far from Tarrytown. By then I was freezing. I was still disproportionately affected by cold, and James was worried about me. There was this raging look in his eyes, like he wanted to punch something. "I can't goddamn believe I forgot to fill up the tank," he said.

He looked at me. "You're shivering."

"Jims," I said through chattering teeth, "I'm fine."

"I can't be trusted with anyone."

"That's not true. I'm just cold. I'm not going to die. Things happen." I put my hand on his shoulder, but he shook me off.

His reaction seemed so out of proportion to the situation. We were only forty-five minutes from home for God's sake. I'm ashamed to say it, but I was a little embarrassed to see James so—I really hate to say this—weak.

When Dad showed up, he didn't seem all that mad about it, but it's hard to tell with my dad sometimes. When we got back to my house, he asked to speak with James outside.

I stood at the window and listened to him.

Dad gave James a speech about how I was still "delicate" (which made me sound edible or like a glass figurine), and that James needed to be *more responsible* with me if he was going to keep seeing me. While I knew that James was already aware of everything Dad had said, I also knew that Dad needed to say it.

"Naomi," Dad said when he came back inside, "I'm worried, kid. James seems a little out of control."

"He's fine," I insisted, a little too adamantly, I suspect. "He's under stress from all the college stuff."

Dad looked me in the eyes. "I want you to know that I trust you."

James had been planning to go visit USC for a tour on the Thursday after his car ran out of gas. He called me the night before he was scheduled to leave.

"I don't know if I can go," he said.

I asked him why not.

"I don't feel right."

"Jims, your car broke down. It was no big deal. Nothing's happened."

"It didn't break. It ran out of gas because *I* forgot to fill it."

"That could happen to anybody—"

"And it's not just that. There was that fight and getting suspended. And . . . and I got fired from my job, I didn't want to tell you, I'd missed too much work."

"What do I care about your job? You were going to have to quit in a couple of months anyway."

"My mom's worried, and even you seem different. The way you looked at me on Sunday night. I've seen girls look at me that way before. I didn't like to see it from you."

"The way I looked at you was only worry because you seemed upset. And I'm not different," I insisted. "I love you. Look, if you get there and you're miserable, I'll come. I promise."

"Your dad would never let you."

"I won't tell him. I'll make something up, I swear. I'll tell him I'm going to a yearbook conference or to visit my mom or something."

"You'd do that for me?"

"Christ, Jims, I threw myself down a flight of stairs just to meet you, didn't I?" It was a joke between us, but he didn't laugh.

"Okay," he said finally. "Okay, but I'm holding you to that."

I didn't hear from him for about a day, but I figured that was probably a good thing. It meant he was busy and having a good time. He called me Friday night.

"How's it going?" I asked.

"I need you to come."

"What's wrong?"

He hadn't even gone down to USC yet. It sounded like all he'd done since he'd gotten to California was sit in his dad's house. "I'm just having a little trouble getting started is all."

But it was more than that. There was something in his voice that scared me. "Are you all right?" I asked.

He didn't answer my question. "Here's the thing," he said. "I looked it up. You can fly out of JFK tomorrow morning. I'd pay for the ticket. All you'd have to do is come."

I found myself saying yes. I threw a couple of T-shirts, my laptop, a few randomly chosen CDs (I'd misplaced my iPod), my headphones, and another pair of jeans into my backpack.

I knocked on Dad's door; he was on the phone, but he got off right away.

Despite the fact that I had been lying for a month, I am not a good liar. My stories are too elaborate and I forget them halfway through; I stammer; I sweat; I smile too much; I don't make eye contact; I make too much eye contact. On this day, I was just right. "Dad," I said, "I forgot to tell you that I'm supposed to go to a yearbook conference in San Diego tomorrow. I'll be back Tuesday." I was glad I hadn't ever told him about quitting yearbook.

Dad didn't even blink. "Do you need any money? A ride to the airport?"

I took the money; I got a ride from Alice and Yvette. Alice had just broken up with Yvette for the second time since the play had ended.

"Cookie, are you sure you know what you're doing?"

"He sounded bad, Alice."

"If he sounded bad, maybe you should have called his mother?" Yvette suggested.

"She just makes things worse," I said.

When we got to the airport, Alice got out of the car to hug me.

"Listen, cookie, we love James, too, but do any of us really know him even?"

"I do!"

"Okay, okay, if you're sure."

"Call us when you get there, Nomi," Yvette said from the car.

I was anxious as hell while I was waiting to get on the plane.

My anxieties flipped between ten or so major issues, many of which also fell under the subheading "if the plane crashes":

1) I hadn't ever flown alone before.

2) If the plane crashed, Dad wouldn't even know I was on it since he thought I was going to San Diego for a yearbook conference.

3) If the plane crashed, Dad's last thoughts about me would be that I was a liar.

4) I didn't pack enough clothes, especially socks and underwear.

5) If the plane crashed, I still wouldn't be speaking to my mother.

6) If the plane crashed, there was a sister who would never know me.

7) James.

8) If the plane crashed, I would still be in a fight with Will.

9) If the plane crashed, I would never "dazzle" Mr. Weir. I would be "incomplete" for all eternity.

10) I hadn't brought anything to read.

I figured I could fix the last one at least, so I went into the nearest airport bookstore.

On a table toward the middle of the store, they had Dad's book, which was just out in paperback. *Out Wandering: A Memoir.* I turned the book over and read the copy. "From the celebrated writer who along with his wife, Cassandra Miles-Porter, brought you the best-selling *Wandering Porters* travel series comes this deeply personal memoir about the end of his marriage, as seen through the prism of world events . . ." blah, blah, blah ". . . how he and his daughter managed to find peace of mind even while . . ." blah, blah, blah ". . . and in some ways, we are all out wandering . . ." blah, blah, blah. It sounded dreadful. I read Dad's bio at the bottom. "Grant Porter lives with his daughter, Naomi, in Tarrytown, New York." I added a couple phrases of my own, "his daughter, Naomi, who is a low-down, rotten liar and who has been lying to him for weeks."

As a pointless act of contrition, I brought the book to the counter, and with the money the author himself had just given me, I bought a copy.

I landed in California around ten in the morning. Even though he had arranged my flight, James was two hours late picking me up.

He hugged me hard when he saw me.

"Jims, you were supposed to be here two hours ago."

"Traffic," he said with a vague wave of his hand. "It's just L.A. I'm so goddamn happy that you're here." And he did look happy, better than before he'd left. His eyes were bright.

We got in the car; I had been planning what I would say to him since we'd gotten off the phone. The idea was to move James in positive directions; the dangerous thing, in my mind, was inertia. "So I thought we could maybe start with taking a campus tour?"

"Is that what you want to do?" he asked.

"Well, I've never seen USC before, and isn't that kind of the point of why you're here?"

"I . . . I guess so. I thought we could go to the beach, maybe go surfing. I've been wanting to take you surfing as long as I've known you. We could take the tour tomorrow, right? I think I'd prefer that."

"Okay," I said.

So we drove to the beach, but on the way I started feeling a little queasy. By the time we got there, I was really ready to get out of the car.

"Christ," James said right after he'd parked.

"What is it?"

"I should have picked up the surf gear from my dad's before we came here."

"It's fine. Let's just sit awhile, okay? I'm feeling kind of green, you know?"

James sat down next to me on the beach, but I could tell he was feeling antsy. He kept drawing these circles in the sand with his right index finger. Finally he jumped up. "Why don't I drive back to my dad's house, and you wait here? I'll come back with the gear and lunch, too."

"How long will you be?"

"Probably about an hour."

I agreed. I'd been traveling for hours, and I was in no mood to get back in that car.

The beach was deserted, and it was a little too cold for beachgoers. The air was crisp and salty. The sand was different from the kind you find on the East Coast: softer, but also firmer somehow. I fell asleep.

I only awoke because a couple were having a picnic on the sand near me. It seemed odd that they would have chosen to be so close to me when they could have sat anywhere, but whatever. He was about forty-five and she was probably ten years younger than that. The guy had gone all-out. He had brought the bottle of wine, the checkered blanket, a stereo with some guy singing opera, roses, and a picnic basket. It was kind of sweet, really. You could tell he'd put a lot of effort into it.

"Sorry," she called out to me, "did we wake you?"

I shook my head. "It's fine. Would you happen to have the time?" I'd left my backpack in James's car.

"About four," she called.

"Thanks." James had been gone for about two and a half hours. Maybe he'd just gotten stuck in traffic again? He couldn't call me; no one could. My phone was in my backpack in his car.

I decided not to panic. I would just lie back down on the beach and wait it out. I really wished I'd taken my bag, because at least then I would have had my headphones.

Another two or so hours later, it was dark, the picnickers were packing up to leave, and James was still not there. "Can we offer you something to eat?" the man called out to me. I figured he probably thought I was a street kid. "We brought way more than we could ever finish."

I shook my head. I wasn't at all hungry. I was too worried about James to be hungry. "I'm fine. I'm just waiting for someone."

The man nodded at me sympathetically. "You shouldn't keep a lady waiting," he said.

"Damn right," the woman said.

Still, before they left, the woman gave me the remains of their Caesar salad and half a carton of strawberries. "Just in case he's too much longer, right?"

I didn't touch the food. Looking at it made me want to weep.

I was terrified for James, of course, but thoughts of self-preservation began to creep into my brain. I wondered what I should do if James never came back. Who should I call? Alice, maybe? My mother? Not Dad. He'd worry too much. And I couldn't bear telling him I'd lied. Maybe Will? Then I started to wonder where the nearest phone was. I didn't even know that much about my location. Somewhere on the Pacific coast near L.A., I reckoned. That narrowed it down to roughly a thousand different places.

Just as I was about to enter all-out panic mode, James appeared. He was carrying a paper bag from a burger place.

"It got cold," he said. "So I had to throw out the first bag and get another."

I didn't even eat hamburgers, but I guess he didn't know that. I jumped up and hugged him and kissed him all over his face.

"I'm sorry," he said. Even in the dark, I could tell his eyes were bloodshot. "I . . . I tried to call you. Your phone was off."

"It was in your car," I said.

"Oh, right."

"Looks like you already ate," he said, pointing to the picnic remains.

"Some people felt sorry for me," I said. "They thought I was homeless."

"Are you mad?" James asked. "Please don't be mad."

"Only the smallest amount. Mainly, I was scared for you."

James sat down on the beach next to me. After a while, I sat down, too.

"I'm sorry," he whispered. "I'm such a goddamn loser."

"No, you're not," I said.

"I am. I am. I am."

"James, don't say that," I said.

He pulled up his knees and set his head on them so that I couldn't see his face.

"James, would you look at me?"

But he wouldn't. It was awkward, but I tried to put my face under his so that he would have to look at me. He still wouldn't move. I kissed the back of his neck. Then I kissed his arm.

After a while, he raised his head. He'd been crying.

"What happened anyway?" I tried to say this gently, but an array of other emotions was diluting my intent.

"I was driving to my dad's in Westwood to get the gear. And I happened to notice this cemetery, so I decided to stop. Marilyn Monroe's buried there. I'd been there before, but this time when I went I noticed how pink the marble on her grave is because people kiss it and touch it so much, you know . . . And that made me depressed as hell. My brother's buried like a mile from there in this other cemetery. No one ever kisses and touches his grave, because no one gives a crap about him, do you know? He was just some kid who died. And it's gonna sound so screwed up, but I drove over to his grave next. I couldn't even find it at first. I'd forgotten where it was. It's way in the back. And I started kissing it, and touching it to try to change the color of the stone . . . I knew it was crazy even while I was doing it, but I've been thinking about him a lot lately. He was never even as old as I am now, how messed up is that? It makes me crazy sometimes.

"This thing I have . . . this depression . . . I can see it coming on. It's like when you're surfing. You want to stay on the crest of the wave as long as possible, but the nature of waves is that they always come back down."

I put my arm around him. James felt so small to me. "I love you," I said.

James laughed, which was horrible. "I can't help but wonder if you'd still say that if you could remember everything. If you were in your right mind."

I could have told him then, but it didn't seem the place. "Don't you love me?" I asked.

"I do."

"Let's get out of here, okay?"

When we got to the car, James looked really tired, so I suggested that if he gave me directions, I could drive.

"I thought you didn't remember how," he said.

"I remembered," I answered. He didn't question me beyond that.

James's dad's house was the California equivalent of James's mom's house. Roomy, empty. His dad was away somewhere. "On business," James said.

"Have you been here by yourself the whole time?"

James shrugged.

I made eggs, but James didn't really eat anything. He didn't say much the whole evening. I could tell he was thinking about something, and I didn't want to disturb him. Still, I felt like each second he didn't speak became an inch between us.

Around ten, he said he was going to bed. I followed him into his room.

I kissed him.

"I need to get some sleep," he said. "I haven't slept in days and days."

"Why not together?" I asked. I knew it was probably pathetic, but I was trying to pull him back to the surface. I loved him even more now that he seemed so vulnerable. Maybe I loved him more because he needed me.

James shook his head. "Naomi," he said sweetly. "Naomi . . . I wish I could."

He took my hand. His grip wasn't very strong at all. He led me into one of the guest rooms.

"Good night," he said, and then he closed the door.

I hadn't turned on my phone since boarding the plane.

There were twenty-eight messages. I was just about to check them when the phone rang. It was Dad. I knew the jig was up.

"Hello," I said.

Here's how it played out:

He'd been trying to phone me all day.

He got worried when I didn't pick up.

He called Will.

He wasn't there, but he got Mrs. Landsman.

Mrs. Landsman didn't know anything about a conference in San Diego. Furthermore, she told him I'd quit yearbook months ago.

He called James's mom.

She said that James was in California.

"I just want to know one thing, is that where you are?"

"Yes," I said, and then I started to cry. It was the tension of the day more than the trouble I was in. It was the sound of my dad's voice. It was lying, not just to Dad but to everyone. It was wondering how I'd let everything get so screwed up. With James and Mom and Will and Dad and school and yearbook and tennis and even poor Ace. It was all the things I hadn't said, but couldn't and wanted to. They constricted my throat to where the only thing to do was cry or choke. It was that half-eaten carton of strawberries and the coin toss that I'd lost and being abandoned in a typewriter case and then again by my own crazy, beautiful, treacherous, wall-painting mother. It was my sunglasses, which I'd left on the beach that day. The sun had gone down and I hadn't needed them anymore. It's when you don't need something that you tend to lose it.

It was James. Of course it was James. He had said I'd looked at him "funny," but I had eyes: he was looking at me that way, too.

Dad booked me on a flight that left at noon the next day, the first one he could find.

In the morning, James looked better. "Maybe I just needed a good night's sleep?"

I told him my dad had found out and that I had to go home.

"I know," he said. "Raina called me. Your dad probably hates me now."

"You're not the one who lied," I said.

On the way to the airport, James took a detour. He drove to USC, where we took the tour.

"It's a step," I said.

"An infinitesimal one," he added. "I still have a lot to work out."

I held his hand the whole time. It was a really beautiful campus, and the sun was out so bright and lovely, it could almost make you forget things.

At the airport, he kissed me, but I tasted goodbye in it.

"I'll see you when you get back to school on Tuesday," I said. "Assuming my dad ever lets me out of my room again."

A security officer yelled at James to move his car, so he had to go. Part of me was scared I'd never see him again.

When I got to the doors of the terminal, I realized that I had left my dad's book in James's car.

Ten

ON THE FLIGHT BACK, I ALTERNATED BETWEEN WORRYING about James and worrying about the trouble I was in, probably about seventy-five percent in the James direction. In lieu of thinking, I would have preferred to be sleeping, but planes are one of the noisiest "in theory quiet" places on earth, and I couldn't.

I put on my headphones and placed a CD in my laptop's drive. I hadn't really noticed what I was packing when I'd left the house, but I'd managed to grab not one but two of Will's stupid mixes. The first one I put in was the one he'd made me when I'd lied to him about the play, but something about it made me anxious. (Maybe it was the song choice; he had, after all, been pissed at me at the time.) So I put in a different one instead, the one from my birthday, *Songs for a Teenage Amnesiac*, Vol. II. A prompt came up on my computer, asking me if I wanted to launch the DVD player.

I clicked yes.

It was a movie, no more than fifteen minutes long.

To call it a movie would probably be an exaggeration. It wasn't in the least professional, not like James's video installations for the play, for example. It was a simple slideshow, set to the Velvet Underground song "That's the Story of My Life." He'd added some text, but mainly it was pictures.

It was all the years I had missed. He had gotten whatever videos and images he and the school and even Mom (yes, he had contacted my mother) possessed, and he had edited them together chronologically.

There I was.

There I was graduating from the lower school at Tom Purdue. I'm easy to spot. I'm the tallest girl in the picture.

And Mom giving birth to Chloe. *My sister.* I knew I hadn't been there that day, and yet it was undeniable: there I was.

And moving with Dad to the new house—our whole life in boxes. And Ace pulling my ponytail on the tennis courts. And me taking a picture of someone taking a picture of me. It was Will—of course it was Will—I could see him dimly reflected in my camera lens.

And in that black formal dress. My hair had been dirty blond, but you could see the roots even then.

Nothing all that thrilling, I guess, but there I was.

There I was, there I was.

As soon as it was finished, I played it again.

And then, I played it again.

How surreal to see my whole life, as compiled by Will, from a plane ten thousand feet in the air.

He'd obviously done it before I had my memory back—he still

didn't know I had my memory back. It must have taken him a lot of time to assemble. It was probably the nicest, most thoughtful gift anyone had ever given me, and I hadn't even bothered to look at it for three months. No wonder he'd been mad at me. I was a jerk, unworthy of the effort.

I spent the next three hours feeling horrible. I tried to use the phone on the back of the seat to call Will, but I couldn't get it to work.

As soon as the plane landed, I turned on my cell, but the battery was dead. I knew that Dad would be waiting for me outside the security checkpoint, and that would effectively mark the end of my freedom for some time. I stopped at the nearest pay phone. I didn't have any change, so I had to call Will collect.

"I have Naomi Porter on the line. William Landsman, will you accept charges?" asked the operator.

"Why not?" was Will's reply. "Well, what do you want?"

"I'm sorry about having to call collect," I began. "My phone died."

"Fine."

"I . . . I got your birthday present. I mean, I got it before, but I hadn't watched it until today. I just wanted to say that it meant a lot to me." The words weren't coming out right. They sounded so stiff and not at all what was in my heart.

"Well . . . Well, that's fine. Do you need something else? I'm on my way out actually."

"Will, I—"

"What?" he snapped. "I'm going out with Winnie."

"Yearbook Winnie? Winnifred Momoi from yearbook?"

"Yes, Winnie Momoi. I've been seeing her since the beginning of the semester. You're not the first person in the world to have a significant other."

"Goodbye, Coach."

"See you." He hung up the phone first.

I went out into the lobby to meet Dad. I felt like the sole of a very old shoe.

The first thing Dad did was hug me, and the second thing he did was ask me for my cell phone.

"It's dead," I told him as I handed it over.

"It's staying that way, kid." He put my phone in his pocket. "I've never had to really punish you before, and I'm not even sure I know how to do it."

"Phone's probably a good start," I said.

"And no regular phone either, or not much." Dad took my backpack and didn't speak to me again until we were in the car.

On the highway Dad elaborated on his plans for my punishment. He told me I was "seriously grounded" for at least the next month. "What's a serious grounding entail anyway?" Dad asked.

"Not sure," I said.

"Not going out with James or anyone else, I think," Dad said. "Also, I want you home immediately after school, and I'll drive you there and pick you up, too."

"I could walk and save you the bother," I said.

"No, this is part of the trust thing. You see, I don't trust you anymore."

It stung, but I deserved it.

"Why didn't you tell me you'd quit yearbook?" he asked.

"I don't know."

"What am I supposed to do with you, Naomi? I never thought I'd see the day that you'd run off to California without telling me. That's after-school special stuff."

"I know."

"Can you tell me anything that will help explain this?"

"I was worried about James," I began. "I could tell he was in a bad place . . ."

"Why didn't you come to me? Didn't you think I would help?"

"It wasn't just James, Dad. It was me, too . . ."

I told Dad everything.

I told him about *remembering* everything.

"Aw, kid," he said, "why didn't you say?"

"I guess my life seemed to be going one way, and it seemed too difficult to think about starting all over again or going backward. And I . . . I didn't want to lose James." I didn't add that I felt like now I had anyway.

"I'm not sure I understand. Why would you have lost James?" Dad asked quietly.

"Because . . . maybe it won't make any sense to you, but not having pasts was something we had in common." It hurt me to even say this next part. "I think it might have been one of the main reasons he liked me."

"I doubt that very much." Dad smiled for a second and then he sighed. "You can drive again?"

I nodded.

"Shame about you being grounded, then."

I didn't talk to James until Tuesday night, when he got back to Tarrytown. I probably wouldn't have even gotten to talk to him then except that Dad had left me alone for about ten minutes, so that he could go get coffee.

We didn't discuss L.A. or anything that had happened there. To tell you the truth, I was overjoyed just to hear from him. I had been worried he might not make it back from California at all.

He didn't say anything at first, but I knew it was him.

"I can't stay on the phone long, Jims," I said finally. "I'm not even supposed to be on the phone now."

He apologized and then he got even quieter—so quiet, I could hear Raina watching TV in her bedroom, and the fridge making ice, and Raina's cat, Louis, lapping water from his bowl. When James did finally speak, his voice was so strange. He asked me, "What do you know about yourself for certain?"

I said, "My name." I laughed to let him know I was done discussing the matter.

He must have taken it like a dot-dot-dot instead of the period I had intended, because he continued, "Besides your name. Besides your name, besides the facts, what do you know about yourself to be true, essentially true?"

Normally, I liked his . . . I guess you'd call it philosophy, but on this night it was sort of scaring me.

I told him that I loved him, because it was all I could think to say.

"I wonder," he said. "I just really wonder. If you knew everything, would you still feel the same?"

I should have just confessed that I did, in fact, know everything, but I didn't.

Then he said, "How do you know that being in love with me wasn't some grand mental delusion?"

I felt insulted, like he was saying that everything that had happened between us didn't count for anything. I took it the wrong way, and I didn't say what I wish I had said, something like, "Love is love. It's not about knowing, and besides, I know everything I need to know anyway."

Instead, I told him I had to go; Dad would be back any minute, and I was in so much trouble already.

Then in a clear, strong, reassuring voice, he said he loved me, too (that too still smarts), and that he'd see me in school the next day, which ended up being a lie.

At lunch, I called his cell phone from the school pay phone. Raina answered. "Naomi," she said, "I was about to call you. It's been a hectic day." Her voice was scratchy and raw, as if she'd been up all night talking.

"Is something the matter with James?" Given James's history, all manner of horrific possibilities came to mind.

"No," she said. "No, he's fine."

Then she told me. James had voluntarily decided to go back to Sweet Lake, which was the Albany mental health facility he'd been in a year ago.

"Why?" I asked. "He was fine."

"I think that he was feeling a bit overwhelmed" was all she said at first.

"He was fine."

"And he basically is fine, but he didn't want things to get bad. They have before for him, you know. It's good, honey, he's trying to be responsible." She said that it might only be for a couple of days, and that he was in the transitional facility, not the full-on psych ward or something. The difference was that at the transitional facility, he could still keep up with his schoolwork and make phone calls. "It's really just a house, Naomi," she said. "He'll probably call you in a couple of days once he's settled in."

I was numb, but underneath that numbness was an indignant little tumor. I couldn't believe he would take off without even telling me himself.

A week passed without any word from James.

I decided that if he wouldn't call me, I would call him. There were things he should know and things I needed to say. So whenever Dad was working or out, I would phone Sweet Lake.

I called him maybe thirty times over the next three days, but he never called me back. There wasn't a direct line to his room or anything. Eventually, I put it to the receptionist point-blank, "Is he getting my messages?" The receptionist sighed or sniffed very heavily—over the phone, this sounds like the same thing—and replied, "Yes. He's getting your messages, but sometimes a patient doesn't feel up to returning a call."

Screw that. I would go see him myself.

I hadn't forgotten my promise to him. I hadn't forgotten his "rules." But I didn't want him locked up without knowing the truth:

I hadn't been with him because I was delusional or an amnesiac. I had loved him. I think I really had.

And screw James. They were his rules, not mine.

Not to mention, I'd had my fingers crossed.

I knew Dad wouldn't let me drive up to Albany by myself and especially not to visit James.

I called Will. "Coach," I said. I knew I was laying it on a bit thick with the "coach" bit, but I needed Will to be in as good a mood as possible.

"What do you want?" Will asked.

"So the thing is," I said, "I sort of need you to drive me to Albany tomorrow."

"Why in God's name would I do that?" he asked.

"I don't know." And I didn't. It had basically been a Hail Mary. I'd been a jerk to Will. So I told him goodbye and I started to hang up the phone.

"Wait a second. I didn't say I wouldn't do it yet."

"Okay."

"What's in Albany?"

I told him.

He lowered his voice. "Honestly, Naomi"—he'd stopped calling me Chief ever since I'd quit yearbook, and now that I had my memory back and could remember what good friends we'd been, it stung—"don't you think I have better things to do on a Saturday than drive you to see your crazy boyfriend?"

"Yes. I'm sure that you do." I wanted to add that James wasn't crazy, but I knew by Will's question that he was coming round.

"I have a yearbook to run. By myself, I might add."

"I know."

"And a girlfriend now."

"Yes." I'd seen him and Winnie Momoi. Everyone said how cute Winnie and Will were together. Even their names were alliterative.

"Well, I just wanted to make sure you appreciated that my whole life doesn't revolve around you anymore," he said. "You'll pay for gas. And meals. And incidentals."

"Incidentals? Like what?"

"Like . . . like sundries and vitamins and pens. Like I don't know like what. I was just on a rhetorical roll. Incidentally, how long does it take to get to Albany?"

"Two hours, I think."

"Okay, that's two CDs. I gotta get started on a mix for tomorrow. Because even though I'm driving you, I'm still not speaking to you, Naomi."

I decided not to point out the obvious: that he was, in fact, speaking to me.

I heard him flipping through his CDs in the background. "*Songs for Visiting Naomi's Crazy Boyfriend in Albany.*" Will and his mixes.

"Catchy title," I told him.

"I'm gonna fill it with all the famously mad and/or suicidal recording artists. Jeff Buckley. Elliott Smith. Nick Drake. And maybe a couple love songs, too. But the really, exquisitely tortured kind."

"There's one other thing," I told Will. "I need you to call my dad and tell him that it's something I have to do for yearbook."

"Christ, Naomi, I am not going to lie for you."

"Please, Will . . . He'll believe you. I can't go otherwise."

"He knows you quit," Will said after a moment.

"I know. Just say it's something I committed to before that only I can do."

"I'll think about it. I'm not promising anything. Not to mention, I don't like the idea of lying to your dad."

That night, Will called my dad and told a very short story about my having agreed to photograph the Special Olympics.

Dad didn't question Will. Everyone knew that William Blake Landsman was no liar. Besides, I think Dad could tell I needed to get out of the house.

We left at noon on Saturday. Mainly I pretended to sleep in the car. I was too nervous to even talk to Will.

When we got there, Will told me he would wait in the car.

"I need you to come in with me," I said.

"Why? Are you scared?"

"No . . . well, I think there's a small chance that he might not want to see me, so I need you to give your name at the desk."

"He doesn't know you're coming?" Will was incredulous.

"Not exactly," I admitted.

"Congratulations. This sounds exceedingly well planned," Will said as he opened his door.

I had expected a prison, but Sweet Lake reminded me of Thomas Jefferson's house, Monticello, where I had taken a field trip in fourth grade. Or maybe it looked like a very large B&B.

Visiting hours on Saturday lasted from noon to seven. I had called ahead. It had been that same receptionist, and I'm pretty sure he recognized my voice because he said, "You do know that patients have the right *not* to see someone."

Will gave his name at the desk, and then we went to wait in the visiting room.

"Will," James said, coming through the door. "Is something wrong with . . . ?" Then he saw me. At first, I thought he was going to walk right back through those doors the same way he'd come, but he didn't.

He walked to the sofa where Will and I were. After a while, James sat down, but he wouldn't look at me.

When he finally did look at me about five minutes later, it was not in a very pleasant way at all. "So?" he said.

I had rehearsed what I wanted to say ever since I'd decided to come. I took a deep breath.

I thought about asking Will to leave, but I didn't. "I think you"—I turned to James; I didn't care if he wanted to look at me or not—"have gotten the idea that if I could remember everything, I wouldn't want to be with you. And since that is the case, I shouldn't be ruining my life by being with you in the meantime when you're so . . . flawed. Is that right?"

He nodded and muttered under his breath, "Something like that."

"Well, here's the thing. I haven't been an amnesiac since January. I love you now. It's not gratitude or amnesia. It's *love*. And I know you're screwed up. Everyone is screwed up. I don't care."

"You're a goddamn liar," James said.

"I can't believe it," Will said. "How could you not say?"

I looked at Will.

"I don't know. I'm sorry."

His face was flushed. "I'll wait for you by the car," he said. And then he left.

James didn't speak to me for a long time. Finally, he said, "Let's go outside. I can't be in here anymore."

It was a nice day, and I don't mean that it was sunny either. It was humid and not too cool, like winter was getting annoyed with itself and wanted it to be spring just as much as everyone else. We sat down at a picnic table.

I remember wanting to touch him, but not feeling like he would let me. Eventually he took my hand. "It's cold," he said. He cupped his hands, which were dry and warm, around mine.

"Sometimes," he said after a while, "I was sort of jealous of your amnesia, I know how crazy that probably sounds. Because for so long in my life, I just wanted to forget everything that had ever happened to me . . .

"After my brother died, it became real easy to picture myself dying young. But recently I've realized that I'm probably not going to unless I do something to make that happen. I know this probably seems evident to you, but it's, well, it's news to me. And if I'm not going to die young, that means I'm stuck with the consequences of my actions. That means I have to figure things out, do you know?"

I did.

"Because now, I'm older than my brother ever was. And I'm going to go to college, which is something that he never did. The way I see it, now's a really good time for me to get a handle on all of this.

"As for you . . . well, I just don't want you to turn into another Sera," he said. "But you make things difficult for me.

"I wish we'd met some other time," James said. "When I was

older and had my shit together. Or younger, before everything got so messed up.

"Someday," he said, "we'll run into each other again, I know it. Maybe I'll be older and smarter and just plain better. If that happens, that's when I'll deserve you, Naomi. But now, at this moment, you can't hook your boat to mine, 'cause I'm liable to sink us both."

I promised to leave him alone until he got out. And then I couldn't help it, I asked him when that might be. I'm ashamed to reveal this, but I might have been thinking a little about junior prom in May.

He said that since he was just in the "transitional" program, he was doing his schoolwork over e-mail and that he hoped to be back for graduation, maybe sooner, but he wasn't sure.

"I'm . . . well, I'm glad to see you, but I'm embarrassed that you're here in a way," he said. "I kind of wanted you to think I was perfect."

I told him that I knew he wasn't perfect.

"Yeah, but I wanted you to think that I was."

We sat on that picnic table for a really long time, until the world became darker and darker. For a second I wished that time might stop, and it might stay twilight forever. Maybe I could live my whole life on this park bench with James, who I loved, next to me.

The sun went down.

Visiting hours were over.

I kissed him goodbye, and Will and I drove back home.

Will didn't talk to me for the first hour and a half on the way back, and when he finally did speak, it was only to alert me to the fact that he wanted to stop at a diner.

"I just want to remind you that I am at liberty to order whatever I want on the menu," he said.

All he ordered was a patty melt and a chocolate milk shake, which was lucky because I only had forty bucks on me and that had to get gas, too. I didn't feel like eating, so I just watched him.

"So . . . so . . . if you've had your memory back all this time, does that mean you remember everything?"

I looked at him. "Yes."

"*Everything* everything?"

I was pretty sure he was thinking of that time he and I had kissed, but I didn't necessarily want to talk about it just then. "Yes."

Will nodded and ate a couple of French fries.

"But that day I made you go back for the camera? Normally, I would have just gotten it myself. I was only being so difficult because I didn't want you to think that things had changed between us. I guess I was overplaying the friends thing."

"It wasn't your fault," I said. "I was the one who tripped."

Will nodded. "I was hurt," he said. "That day, I can truly say I was hurt. I was in love with you, and the next day you acted like us kissing was no big thing."

"Will . . ." I sighed. "Of course, it was a big thing. How could it not have been? You're my best friend, right?"

"I know I should have said something, right then in the parking lot, but by the time I had a chance, you'd forgotten everything. Me entirely. Then you quit yearbook. You met James. It was all too late. But the worst of it is, somewhere in there . . . somewhere after you and that idiot Zuckerman broke up, maybe I had a chance? But I didn't say anything then either.

"But I don't love you anymore," he said firmly.

"Will."

"I don't love you so much."

I couldn't figure out anything to say. In a way, I sort of wished I was in love with him instead of James, because it would have been easier on everyone.

Eleven

THE FOLLOWING WEEK, I GOT A POSTCARD FROM JAMES.

First off, the picture made me laugh, but he probably knew that it would. Big-eyed, cherubic, blond cartoon toddlers (were they brother-sister, or were they more?) on the beach, and the caption at the bottom, *Wish You Were Here . . . Albany, NY.* Are there even beaches in Albany? And considering where *here* was for him, I doubt he actually wished I was *there*.

Then I flipped the postcard over and read his personal message, which was only two words long and had no signature. "Forget me," he wrote. That was it, that was all.

It seemed like the worst possible thing a person who knew me at all would ask.

Yes, I would leave him alone.

No, I would not forget him. It wasn't his choice.

The only person I wanted to talk to about all this was Will.

I tried him on the phone, but he wasn't picking up. I ran to school—the exertion felt strangely good—and he was still in the yearbook office, but he was talking to Winnie Momoi. I didn't want to go in and interrupt, so I waited in the hallway for him or Winnie to leave. I guess he must have seen me through the window on the yearbook door. He came outside like fifteen seconds later, and I burst into tears, even though I could see Winnie watching us curiously.

I could tell he wanted to ask me what was wrong, but he didn't. He put his arm around me, and we started walking out to his car.

The only thing he said to me was "You're not wearing your coat." He went back into the office and returned with his coat (this crazy orange suede one with a lamb's wool collar) and he told me to put it on. I did. It must have weighed about sixty pounds. It was huge on him, so I was basically drowning in it.

He drove me home.

"It's really over," I said.

"I know," Will said.

"I'm such a jerk," I said.

"No, you're not, Chief. You're great."

Somehow Will calling me great started me crying all over again. I didn't feel at all great.

I wasn't crying for James, though. I think I was crying for how much he didn't know me and how much I didn't know him and how I'd acted like such an idiot. How messed up it was that I didn't feel like I could even tell him when I got my memory back.

I was crying a little for the boy I had wanted him to be and the boy he hadn't turned out to be.

And I was crying for gravity. It had sent me down the stairs, and I'd thought that meant something, but maybe it was just the direction that all things tend to flow.

My heart was a little broken (is there such a thing?), but I still had to go to school. I buttoned my dress shirt over it and my winter coat, too. I hoped it didn't show too much.

A sort of funny thing happened the next afternoon. I was standing at my locker talking to Alice when Will's Winnie confronted me.

Winnie had long dark hair that reminded me of my mom's, and made me miss my old hair a little. My hair was starting to look like crap by the way—it wasn't short enough to be short or long enough to be anything else. I hadn't considered how long it would take to grow out when I'd cut it in the first place.

Back to Winnie. She was five inches shorter than me, but that didn't stop her from getting right up in my face. "Look, Naomi," she said, "he was in love with you. We know it. Everyone knows it. But Will is a person of value, and you threw him out when you had James, so now you should just leave him alone."

"Gauntlet thrown," said Alice. She let out a low-pitched whistle.

I was shocked. Winnie had always seemed so sweet and like the least likely person ever to confront you in a hallway with a "stay away from my man" speech.

I told her that Will and I "are just friends and barely that."

Winnie narrowed her eyes at me before storming off.

"Cookie, do you need me to kick her butt?" Alice asked. "We're about the same height, but I'm fiercer than I look."

I shook my head. Even though Winnie was being absurd and I could have used a friend at that particular moment, I decided to keep my distance from Will. I needed his friendship, but I wasn't sure that I deserved it.

I will

Twelve

I WAS STILL GROUNDED, NOT THAT IT MATTERED anyway. I didn't have anywhere I wanted to go.

To pass the time, I studied, I tried to come up with a new photography project, I ran laps around my neighborhood.

I read my dad's book in its entirety. It was much the way the jacket described it, but there was this one part where he talked about how he had been "emotionally unfaithful" to Mom even before the split. He wrote how he was always flirting, always wanting people to like him, even needing their kid (me) to love him more. He wrote, "At times, it must have been exhausting to be my wife." It was strange to know that my dad had such thoughts.

I listened to music. I went through all of my own CDs first. Then I listened to the CDs Will had made for me, and when I was done with those, I listened to them again. It was a completely different experience, listening to his mixes with my memory back. All the songs meant a little something to me. They were a sort of shorthand between us, a common language that I never could have guessed at. The last song of the first one he'd ever given me (*Songs for a Teenage Amnesiac*, Vol. I) had this song called "I Will" on it. It was sweet and old-fashioned, kind of like him.

About a month into my punishment, Dad got tired of seeing me mope around the house. "I'm letting you out this weekend, kid."

I asked him if that meant the grounding was over.

"Nope," he said. "But I am packing you off to your mother's."

I could have argued, I suppose. I could have put up a fuss, but what was the point? I knew this visit was long overdue.

When I got to her apartment, my mother answered the door. She said she'd sent Fuse and Chloe away for the day so it would just be us.

She smiled very casually. "I thought we could talk about your photography project today. Tell me what it's supposed to be." Her wording seemed a bit canned, like she'd been practicing it for days. Her nervousness touched me, I guess.

We went into Mom's studio and she showed me pictures, her own and other people's, and we tossed some ideas back and forth.

One of Mom's personal albums was a pregnancy album. She had taken a single picture of herself each and every day for eight months. Beginning with the day she found out "for certain" from the doctor, she had fastened one of her cameras to a tripod and positioned it in front of a burgundy velvet wingback chair. I remembered the chair from my old house because Dad had always hated it. Also, Mom happened to be sitting in it now as I looked at the album.

Every picture was the same composition—my mother in the

chair—except her clothing changed and her bump got bigger. Here and there, you would find one with Fuse's hand on Mom's belly. There were 225 pictures total. If you stacked them in a pile and shuffled through them really fast, it was a cartoon flip book where nothing much happened aside from the miracle of human life, if you're into that sort of thing . . .

The last one showed a gray sky, with my mother wearing blue jeans and a white V-neck undershirt that I guessed belonged to Fuse. Her expression wasn't one of the obvious ones like happy or sad—it fell somewhere between *greeting a person you haven't seen in a long time* and *stifling a yawn*, but it really wasn't either. You'd probably have to see the picture to know what I meant.

Mom came to look at the album over my shoulder. "These are from ages and ages ago. Before you were even born."

"It's not Chloe, then?" I asked, surprised.

Mom shook her head. There was a faraway look in her eyes. "Your dad and I, we lost that one."

I had never known that. I had thought they couldn't get pregnant. It occurred to me how it was funny all the things you don't know about someone, even someone you live with. How, in a way, the story of that baby was the beginning of my story, wasn't it? Though I never would have known it looking at the pictures, and no one else would ever have known it either. Not unless there'd been a footnote.

That was when I had an idea for my photography project.

Each picture in my series would be a footnote to the next. In other words, all the images would be footnoting each other. The photos would explain each other through other photos.

The first picture I took was a restaging of my "birth." I got a typewriter case from a thrift store and lugged it back to my mother's apartment in New York City. Chloe, although she was not a baby, played the part of me. She couldn't fit in the case, so she stood on top of it.

The next picture I took connected mainly to Chloe. It was a photo of Chloe and me in Mom's velvet chair. I meant that one to represent how we were related, but only through the chair, not by blood. In the front of the frame, I staged it so that you could see Mom's back and a camera tripod.

I took one of a camera sitting at the bottom of the stairs at Tom Purdue. It rained that day, which made the image even more perfect. At first, I thought that one was about James, but I think it might have been about me.

I took one at that same park in Rye I'd visited with James. I put a typewriter in the middle of a field and a typewriter case as far away as I could while still keeping the two objects in the same frame. This one was about Will, I suppose. Or you could read it as a footnote to the typewriter case picture.

I staged about twenty-five more pictures. It took the better part of the next month, but I was happy with the results.

When I presented my project in Mr. Weir's class the next week, I was scared at first; those photo kids could be tough.

"When I was younger," I began, "my parents wrote these books. My dad wrote all the text, and my mother took all the pictures, but she also wrote the occasional footnote. That's the only time I'm ever really mentioned in these books. That, and the picture on the back flap. I call my project 'Footnotes from a Lost Youth,' but I'm still playing with the title. It might be a little pretentious . . ."

Mr. Weir gave me a B. "It would have been an A–," he said, "but I had to deduct for lateness." He also put up my pictures in the school's gallery. It was odd to have something so personal out there in that way, but the good thing about art is that no one necessarily knows what you mean by it anyway.

Dad and Rosa Rivera came. So did Alice and Yvette and all the kids I'd been in the play with.

Will came to see my pictures, too. I don't know when, but one day a mix CD showed up in my mailbox, *Footnotes from a Lost Youth*. The first track was "Yoshimi Battles the Pink Robots, Part I," the same one he'd been considering all those months ago. I felt forgiven I called to thank him, but he wasn't home.

Even Mom and Fuse came in from the city to see my pictures.

They took me out to dinner afterward. Of all things, what we talked about was how they had met.

The first time was in high school, which I had already known.

Fuse said that the second time was twenty years later on a subway platform in Brooklyn. Mom had been waiting to go to her photography show and Fuse had been waiting on the opposite subway platform to go to Manhattan to meet with clients. Just before Mom's train got there, Fuse wrote his phone number on a sheet of looseleaf paper and held it up so she could see it, but he had no idea if she would write it down or call or what. Then Mom's train pulled out of the station. She was still standing there, fishing through her bag. She yelled across the platform, "I couldn't find a pen." Then Fuse pointed up, meaning that they should meet outside the train station.

"So, depending on how you look at it, our love story took twenty years or thirty seconds," Mom joked.

"It was very fast or very slow," I said.

"Love stories are written in millimeters and milliseconds with a fast, dull pencil whose marks you can barely see," Fuse said. "They are written in miles and eons with a chisel on the side of a mountain-top."

"Honey," Mom said with amusement in her voice, "that's awfully poetic." She coughed. "Pretentious."

"It's the philosophy major in me." Fuse blushed.

The next week, I went to take down my pictures from the school gallery. When I got to the one of me and Chloe in the chair, it put me in mind of the difference between her origins and mine.

For Chloe, Mom had gone through pain, sweating, and thirty-five extra pounds. But at least she'd only had to travel a couple of blocks from her apartment to the hospital.

For me, she had filled out many forms, crossed her fingers, paid fifteen thousand dollars, overcome a language barrier, and dealt with opportunistic Russian bureaucrats. After all that, she got to sit for thirty hours in coach.

The delivery was different, but the result was basically the same. It was like Fuse had said: a love story in millimeters or a love story in miles.

Thirteen

ACE APPROACHED ME AGAIN ABOUT JOINING THE TENNIS team. His mixed doubles partner, Melissa Berenboim, had torn her ACL. She was out for the last three games of the season, and he needed a replacement quickly. "We never thought we should play together while we were going out, but I figured it's fine now," he said.

"What about our fight and everything else?"

"I thought you might say that, but first and foremost, I have to be a good captain to my team, and what is good for the team is me finding a replacement for Missy. Naomi, there are way, way, way more important things than whatever stupid stuff happened between you and me."

"Like?" I was curious what Ace would say.

"Like tennis. And strong knees."

"I'm warning you, I'm totally out of practice."

"I'll whip you right back into shape, Porter."

The truth was, I'd wanted to go back to the team for a while. I wasn't the greatest player in the world, but I loved playing. Ace had known that about me.

"Sure," I said. "Why not?"

Actually, Ace was a great doubles partner: not selfish, not trying to go for every shot, instinctively knowing when I could reach the ball and when I couldn't. We were a good team. We won more than we lost, which was saying something considering how little practice time we'd had.

We enjoyed each other on the court, too. Like if the score was forty–love, Ace might make a joke and say something like, "Forty— and maybe it's love, but probably not if she dumps you on home- coming night."

"Ha," I said.

One day I wore those tennis sweatbands on the court. I held up my wrists and said to him, "Notice anything special about me?"

Ace whistled and said, "The guy who got those for you must have been some romantic."

It was all sort of corny, but we amused each other. It was easy to remember why I had liked him in the first place.

We were in the athletic department van on the way back from a match when Ace said to me, "I heard about James."

"Yeah," I said, hoping he would leave it at that.

"Maybe you could go up to visit him?"

I told him that I already had, but that we were basically taking some time off from each other.

Ace nodded. He said, "I can tell that you really love him. I know what you look like when you're in love. *I know you.*"

Then Ace apologized. "When we broke up, I might have said some things that weren't very nice about you. I'm sorry for that."

Of course, I had forgiven him ages ago. I told him I was sorry, too. "Things hadn't been going well for a while, had they? Even before my accident, I mean?"

Ace smiled that dopey grin of his and just shook his head.

The third week of May, I was helping Alice paint the sets for her new play, a production of *Hamlet*, when James sauntered into the theater. I hadn't known he'd be back that day.

James was still handsome as ever. Less emaciated and that was good. He asked me if I wanted to go get coffee somewhere. I told him I had to finish painting first, which I did.

At the coffee shop, he told me about Sweet Lake, and I told him about my pictures.

He told me he had quit smoking, and I told him I was letting my hair grow out.

He told me how he'd made friends with a girl called Elizabeth while he was away, and I told him how I had sent Chloe an Emily Dickinson poem last week.

"Which one?" he asked.

" 'I'm Nobody.' It's sort of a nickname she has for me. We read it in Mrs. Landsman's class, so I photocopied it and sent it to her. When I was a kid, I always loved getting stuff in the mail, didn't you?"

James nodded.

Soon after, we ran out of things to talk about.

Our moment had passed somehow. I was different. He was, too.

Without our "madness" (how else to put it?) to unite us, there wasn't anything much there. Or maybe too much had happened in too short a time. It's like when you take a trip with someone you don't know very well. Sometimes you can get very close very quickly, but then after the trip is over, you realize all that was a false sort of closeness. An intimacy based on the trip more than the travelers, if that makes any sense.

Whatever it was, I knew he felt it, too.

He drove me back to my house.

"You still have paint on your palm," he observed. "Like mine, the first time we met."

"Except that was your blood, Jims," I pointed out. "This'll just wash out, you know?"

"True, true. But it healed pretty quick actually." He kissed me on my cheek.

I went to prom by myself, but I ended up hanging out with Yvette and Alice.

The first person I ran into was Ace. His new girlfriend was a tennis player from another school. Ace introduced me in the following way: "This is Naomi Porter, my ex-girlfriend and current mixed-doubles partner."

"Probably more information than you needed," I said to Ace's girlfriend, rolling my eyes.

Will was there with Winnie. He was wearing a powder blue tuxedo, and she looked teeny tiny in a matching powder blue vintage tulle dress with a full skirt. (Personally, I'm too tall for most vintage clothes.) It was a lot of blue, but they looked adorable. Will and I never got a chance to talk. At one point, he winked at me from across the room; I winked back.

He was a good boyfriend to her. He brought her punch, made sure she had a seat when she wanted one, and watched her purse when she went to the ladies' room.

He was a good boyfriend to her as, in some universe elsewhere, he might have been to me.

Fourteen

ROSA RIVERA, MY DAD, AND I WERE WATCHING A nature program. Dad still watched them, though he watched fewer now, and when he did, it was with Rosa Rivera or me.

In any case, this particular one was about porcupines. So the guy porcupine will sing a song if he wants to mate, and if the lady porcupine's not in the mood or would prefer a different porcupine, she pretends not to hear him before running away. And sometimes he's completely the right porcupine, but she'll run away anyway because she's not ready. But if he's the porcupine for her and the timing's right, they stand up and face each other, eye-to-eye and belly-to-belly. They really take the time to *see* each other.

"This is so sweet," Rosa commented. "He is showing her the respect. Why don't you do that to me?" She turned Dad to face her, porcupine-style.

"After the staring has continued an appropriate time," the TV narrator went on, "the male porcupine covers the female from tip to toe with his own urine."

"Please do not ever do that to me, darling," Rosa told Dad.

"His own urine?" Dad asked. "Isn't that redundant? Who else's urine might he be using?"

The TV narrator advised "never getting too near porcupines mating," which seemed like sound, if obvious, advice to me.

I didn't hear what happened after the urination because my cell phone rang, so I went into the dining room to answer it. It was Will's girlfriend, Winnie.

"I was wondering if you'd heard from Will," she said stiffly.

I hadn't spoken to him since lunchtime, which wasn't particularly uncommon since I wasn't on yearbook anymore and we didn't have any classes together. He'd sometimes call me at night, but just as often not. "No," I said. "Why?"

"No one's heard from him since the ambulance came. We thought he might call you."

"Winnie, what are you talking about? What ambulance?"

"You haven't heard, then?" she asked.

Obviously. Why do people always ask that? I said, "No, Winnie. Please tell me."

It had started after school at *The Phoenix*. First he had had a coughing fit and then he said he was having trouble breathing. He tried to continue working, though everyone could tell he wasn't himself. Then he passed out. He woke up right before the ambulance got there. Winnie said that he told everyone to keep working, and that nobody should come with him in the ambulance, and that he'd call with instructions later that night. "Isn't that so like Will?" Winnie asked. "Only he never called in with instructions, which is completely not like him, and now everyone's freaking out. I should have gone with him. I can't get Mrs. Landsman on the phone." Her voice was small. "Do you think he's dying, Naomi?"

"I'm sorry, Winnie, I have to get off the phone now. I'll call you if I hear anything." My hands were shaking.

Dad muted the porcupine program and called out from the living room. "Is everything okay?"

I took a deep breath. I dialed Will's home number, but no one picked up.

"Is everything okay?" Dad had come into the dining room.

"It's Will," I told Dad. "They . . ." I cleared my throat. "They took him away in an ambulance. He's sick. We have to go to the hospital."

Dad looked at his watch. "I'm sure it's nothing serious. Besides, it's nearly ten o'clock, Naomi. They won't let you visit him until tomorrow anyway."

"I have to know what's wrong." I started heading toward the door.

"Wait!" Dad said. "I'll call the hospital first."

While Dad found the number to the hospital and called it, I thought of how Will knew everything about me, and how if he were gone, part of me would be missing forever. I wondered if the person who really loves you is the person who knows all your stories, the person who *wants* to know all your stories.

Dad hung up the kitchen phone and said, "They have a William Landsman, but of course they wouldn't tell me anything about his condition. We can't ring his room because it's too late. But if he has a room, he's definitely not dead, Nomi."

"What if he's dying, Dad? I'm going down there."

Dad sighed. "It's ten o'clock. Visiting hours are over. Besides, it's storming out." There was a particularly brutal late spring downpour going on outside with wind, lightning, and all the special effects.

"Maybe his mom will be in the waiting room? And she could tell us what happened," I argued.

Dad looked me in the eye. "Okay," he said finally, grabbing his keys off the dining room table. "Rosa, we're going out for a bit."

In our rush we had forgotten umbrellas, and Dad and I got completely soaked on the walk from the parking lot to the hospital.

When we got there, the waiting room of the pediatrics unit was completely empty. I whispered to Dad that he should ask the nurse behind the desk if she could tell us about Will's condition. I figured they'd be more likely to respect an adult than a teenage girl. But when the nurse asked if Dad was Will's guardian, Dad shook his head no, like a goddamn idiot.

I burst into tears. My dad could be so annoying.

The nurse looked at me curiously. "I recognize y'all. Head trauma in August, am I right?"

I nodded.

"I pretty much have a photographic memory for faces," she reported. "How you been, hon?"

"Mainly good. Except my friend Will might be dying and no one will tell me anything," I said.

"Oh, honey, he ain't dying. He just has"—she lowered her voice to a whisper—"pneumonia is all. A bad case. His lung collapsed, but he's sleeping now. And *I* didn't just say that."

I leaned across the desk and kissed her once on each of her

cherubic peach cheeks, even though getting physical with total strangers was not my thing at all.

"Thank you," I said. "Thank you, thank you."

"My pleasure," she said. "And *I* didn't just say *that*, either."

"Could I leave a note to let him know I was here?"

"Sure thing, honey." She handed me a piece of hospital stationery.

I didn't know what to write. My heart had been bursting with so many things, and yet, when it came time to put any of them on paper, I couldn't. Finally I wrote the following lines:

Dearest Coach,

I'll see you tomorrow, if you'll have me.

Yours,

Chief

I handed the note to the nurse. I saw her read it before folding it in half and writing Will's name across the other side. "Visiting hours start at eleven," she said.

I remembered how Will had gotten there at 10:50 when it was me in the hospital, and I vowed to do the same.

In the car on the way home, Dad kept stealing sidelong glances at me. "Is something going on between you and Will?"

"No." I shook my head. I wondered if I had said too much in my note. What the hell had I meant by *if you'll have me*? Of course he'd have me. It was a hospital. You got visited by whoever showed up. What was Will, who analyzed everything, going to make of my stupid note? "No," I said firmly.

"You sure?"

"I'm sorry, Dad. I have to make a call," I said by way of changing the subject, but also because I actually did. I dialed Winnie's number. "Winnie? This is Naomi Porter. He's going to be fine," I said.

I knew Dad wouldn't give me permission to skip two periods of school, so I didn't ask. Instead, I forged a note claiming a doctor's appointment (and wasn't that partially true, really? I *was* going to a hospital after all . . .).

In the elevator I thought about the note I had left for Will the night before and how it contained the three most ill-conceived sentences in the history of the world. Why had I written "Dearest Coach"? The "dearest" seemed ridiculously sentimental in the morning. We were talking about Will here. And "Yours, Chief"? Would he think I was saying that I was his and he was mine? Which, incidentally, I had been, but I didn't want him to know that yet.

I tried to put it out of my mind. And maybe he hadn't gotten it anyway? It hadn't exactly been sent registered mail or something.

When I got to his room, he was sitting up in bed with his laptop on his food tray. He was wearing hospital pajamas with his smoking jacket over them, and he looked like himself, but very pale. He smiled at me, and I suddenly felt shy around him.

"Hey there" was all I could manage to say. I didn't make eye contact either. I had my eyes focused on the foot of the bed. Then I decided that this was idiotic, so I looked at him as unsentimentally as possible. "Well, what happened to you?"

I moved over to his bedside and Will told me. He'd been feeling bad for a while, but he'd ignored it, thinking it was stress or just the flu or what have you. And yesterday, all of a sudden, he passed out. "They have no idea how I managed to take it so long," he said almost proudly. "My lung had collapsed, it was so packed with bacteria."

"Lovely," I said.

"Isn't it though? It was much more complicated than your average pneumonia."

"You could never be simple," I said.

We went on like that for a while, not saying all that much. If Will had gotten my note, he didn't mention it or didn't think it was anything to remark on. I didn't bring it up either.

Yet, inside me, things were different. It was like that physics DVD I'd watched about string theory way back when. Do you remember? The one with the scientists groping around in the dark. I had thought the way I felt about Will was just a room, but it had turned out to be a mansion. He had turned out to be the mansion. Now that I knew that, it was difficult to go back to the way things had been.

At the end of my visit, Will told me he needed to talk about something serious. I thought to myself, *Here it comes. My stupid note.*

All he said was "I need you to do me a really important favor."

"Absolutely," I said. "Do you want me to get your assignments or something?"

He shook his head. "No, Winnie's doing that. I want you to run yearbook for me while I'm away. You know as much as me, and I'll probably be out of school for at least the next two weeks. Plus, the book's done. Only distribution and the end-of-year inserts and things like that. Stuff you could do sleepwalking, Chief."

"Sure thing, Coach," I said. "Just put me in the game."

So that's how I went from Ex-Co-editor to Interim Editor-in-Chief of *The Phoenix*.

There were a few people on the staff who were not exactly happy to see me back. They rightfully thought of me as a traitor and a deserter. But most of the staff understood that I was filling in for Will because he had asked me to do it. They didn't necessarily throw a parade, but out of respect for him they respected me.

Will sent me almost hourly e-mails. As his mother had banned him from the phone for the first several days of his recuperation, I went to see him every night with updates and to ask advice, even though it wasn't the sort of work that required much input. It was mainly just accounting and distribution, as Will had said. But he was crazy over that sort of thing.

His seventeenth birthday was June 5.

I did the best I could to wrap the record player, but I hadn't done that great a job and the arm was poking out. I lugged it out to the car, then drove over to the apartment he shared with his mom. Winnie was there, as were Mrs. Landsman and a few people from the staff.

It was a pretty tame birthday party. I was glad of it. He had only been out of the hospital about a week, and I still worried about him. Winnie gave him a straw hat with a black-and-white band that was without question something Will would wear; Mrs. Landsman gave him a pair of binoculars. He left my gift for last, but he kept making jokes about it, like "I wonder what that is . . . Could it be a toaster? A tennis racket?"

When he finally ripped the paper off, he said, "Of course you know I'm perfectly shocked."

"I would have found a box, but I didn't think you could handle too much excitement, Landsman."

Winnie put her arm around Will's shoulders. "Now we have something to play all those records on, baby."

I tried to smile at Winnie, but it stuck in the middle somewhere. "I should go," I said.

"No," Will said, "don't go yet. This is great, Chief." He hadn't called me that in such a long, long time. "When'd you get this?"

"Months ago. Before everything. When Dad first started dating Rosa Rivera, I mentioned to her about your record collection, and she showed up with this crazy old record player. Rosa Rivera's always trying to give stuff away."

"So, it's a re-gift?" Winnie asked.

"No, I had to get it fixed. I was planning to give it to you at the start of the school year—you know, as a way to celebrate us being editors of *The Phoenix*—but the guy at the store had to order a part, and it took longer than I'd hoped. By the time it was finished, I'd forgotten I'd dropped it off in the first place. I only got it back because I happened to be in that same store last November to pick up something else and the store owner recognized me. But then, I didn't even know who it was for."

"You couldn't guess it was me? Who else has vinyl?"

"At the time, I'd forgotten about your record collection. When I remembered, you and I were not exactly speaking."

"That's an amazing story," Mrs. Landsman said. "So much misdirection, rather like a Shakespearean comedy."

Will put on the hat that Winnie had bought him. "Looks good, baby," she said. I didn't like the way she called him baby. Not to mention, if she'd been so concerned about him, why hadn't she noticed that he'd been sick all that time? Maybe I wasn't being fair. I often had such thoughts when I was around Winnie and Will.

"I should go," I said.

"Won't you stay for some cake, Naomi?" Mrs. Landsman asked.

I shook my head. "There're a couple things I have to do for year-book tonight. Tomorrow's the day the book's supposed to arrive at school." D-Day, we called it.

"I should be there for that, Ma," Will said.

"You're staying right here," Mrs. Landsman said.

"But, Mrs. Landsman . . ." Will protested, like a student asking for a better grade.

I shook Will's hand and wished him a happy birthday.

He called me later that night.

"I really loved your gift," he whispered so that his mother wouldn't hear. She had set a phone curfew for him of nine o'clock while he was recuperating, and it was already ten-thirty.

"I'm glad."

"You know those records were my dad's."

"Yes, Will." Of course I knew that; I knew everything about that boy. "But my thinking was . . . It was so long ago . . . My thinking was that maybe you ought to take them off the wall and play them once in a while?"

Will didn't say anything for a minute. "Winnie br—"

At that moment, Mrs. Landsman came on the line. "William Blake Landsman, you are supposed to be asleep."

"Ma!"

"Hi, Mrs. Landsman," I said to my English teacher.

"Hello, dear. Tell my son that he needs to get off the phone, would you?"

What could I do? Certainly I had an interest in whatever Will was planning to tell me about Winnie, but the woman would be grading my final in less than two weeks. "You should rest, Will."

"Thank you," said Will's mother. "Now tell Naomi goodbye and hang up the phone, William."

"Good night, Chief," he said.

The next day was chaotic with the arrival of the books. When I opened the first cardboard box, I felt sadness that Will wasn't there. It had been his baby after all, and it didn't seem right that I should be the first one to see the book, certainly not without Will. No one had loved this yearbook more than he, and all his work had made this beautiful thing that people would have forever. The book was all white. In the lower right-hand corner it said *The Phoenix* in a very simple black Arial type font, and on the spine was a small silver bird coming out of a silver flame. The inside papers were gray, and on the upper left-hand corner of the interior front cover the school's name and date were printed. It was simple and elegant; we had begun the design months, even years earlier, before we had even been co-editors.

Of course, I had to call Will. "I only have a minute. It's about to get crazy here."

"I know," he said wistfully. "I was thinking about walking down—"

"Don't you dare!"

"Well, I decided against it. Even if I did make it there, my darling mother would probably murder me. How does it look?"

"It's gorgeous," I told him. "I'm so proud of you. I'll come to you as soon as we're done getting the books out."

"I'm glad you're there." Will coughed, but even his coughs were sounding so much better. "I was just thinking . . . isn't it lucky that we decided to become co-editors? If one takes a blow to the head, the other can fill in. If the other's lung spontaneously collapses, the one can fill in. It's a perfect system when you think about it."

I laughed. "Hey, Will, I could give the book to Winnie. She'll probably get to you before me. You know how it is on D-Day."

"No, I'd rather you brought it, Chief," he said.

"Or your mom, if you'd prefer. I can send Patten or Plotkin to drop it off in her classroom."

"No," he insisted, "it should be you."

I didn't get over to Will's house until seven-thirty, and by then I was spent. "He's waiting for you," his mother said. She made me promise to leave by nine, so that Will could get his rest. "You look like you could use some, too," she said.

I went into Will's room.

The walls were still lined entirely by his dad's record collection. The record player was sitting on the bureau.

"Okay," Will said, "let's have it."

I handed him the book; he started flipping through each and

every page. He was lying on his stomach on his bed, and I lay down next to him the same way so that I could look at it, too. We would complain about a typo here or the way a picture had printed there, but it wasn't the type of thing anyone except us would even notice. The last thing we looked at was the cover.

"I think we were right to go with the all-white, don't you?"

I nodded. "I love it. Everyone at school did, too."

"You haven't forgotten our joke, have you?" Will smiled at me.

I hadn't. The title in the corner was printed so that it almost looked like a textual orphan. "The orphan," I said.

"Exactly." His voice changed a little. "You won't have forgotten the *White Album* either?"

Our reference in coming up with the whole design had been the Beatles' *White Album*, which had been Will's dad's favorite record. I scanned Will's walls to locate it—he arranged his albums alphabetically by title—but there was a gap in his collection where it ought to have been.

"Where'd it go?" I asked.

He said he'd taken it down, that he wanted it to be the first record he'd played on his new (old) record player. "I was waiting for you to get here."

The album was two records long, and he set it on the turntable on side three (or side one of the second record). He put down the needle.

We listened for a while and kept flipping through the book, occasionally making a comment to each other about something or other.

"I really wish my dad could have seen this," Will said. He took off his glasses and wiped them on his pants.

The second to last track on the third side was called "I Will." When it came on, I pointed out to him how it had been the final song of the first mix he'd made me after my accident. "Had you been trying to remind me about the cover?" I asked.

"Sort of," he said shyly with that funny crooked smile of his, "but I'd been mainly trying to remind you about me. *I, Will*, you know?"

"If you had ever signed my yearbook instead of just leaving that big old blank box, that probably would have done the trick, too," I said.

"S'pose."

"Why didn't you anyway?"

"Too much to say," Will said with a decisive nod of his head. "Too much to say with none of the right words to say it. I'd rather just pick the perfect song to do the work for me."

It was such a sweet, sad song with such sweet, sad lyrics. Old-fashioned a little, but also timeless. I wanted to hear it again nearly as soon as it was over, but by that time it was nine o'clock. I shook Will's hand—was it my imagination or did he hold it longer than was strictly necessary?—then I drove myself home.

By Thursday, most of the yearbooks had been distributed. For the first time in over a week, I had time to go eat with Alice and Yvette, who were back together again.

"We love the book, cookie," Alice said.

"It's mainly due to Will," I said.

"Well, tell him we love the book when you see him," she said.

I said that I would.

"Did you hear that Winnie Momoi broke up with him?" Yvette asked.

"While he's been sick? Did you know about this, cookie?" Alice looked at me.

I shook my head and concentrated on chewing my sandwich.

"Yeah," said Yvette, "she's in my math class, and she was crying all day on Monday."

"Why was she the one crying if she broke up with him?" Alice asked.

"Guilt, maybe? You cry every time you break up with me, Ali."

"Touché," said Alice, and then she changed the subject. "I hate the word *touché*, don't you? I can't imagine what possessed me to say it. It sounds like tushy, or something you say while eating cheese."

"Actually, it's a fencing term," Yvette said. "You'd know if you ever came to my matches."

"I come to your matches!" Alice said. "I've been to at least three."

"Two!"

Their fights often started like this and went on for days. I ignored them and thought about Will instead. I had seen and called him over ten times since Monday, and he had never mentioned anything about Winnie to me. I wondered what had happened between them, but I didn't really feel like it was my place to ask. If he wanted to talk to me about it, I figured that he would. These days, I was careful around Will, and he was careful around me.

Even if we never got together in a romantic way, I loved him. I guess I always had. To tell you the truth, the knowledge was something of a burden.

I remembered those porcupines I'd been watching with Dad the night I thought Will might be dying. Not the part about the urinating. The part where they looked each other in the eye. Will and I weren't there yet. (Personally, I hoped never to get to the peeing stage.)

I stopped by Will's house after school to tell him I wouldn't see him for the next three days—I was taking off Friday to go to Martha's Vineyard for Dad's and Rosa Rivera's wedding. I knew that Will had gotten used to my coming around every day, but I chose my words deliberately. I didn't want him to think that I had any expectation that he would care that I was leaving. I also didn't want to pull another disappearing act on him.

"Your dad's wedding," he said. "It sure came up fast, didn't it?"

"Yeah."

"Well, why didn't you invite me, Chief?" He said this in a cheerful way where I couldn't tell if it was a serious request.

"Well . . . you've been sick, so I doubt your mother would have let you go."

"True, true."

"And also"—I didn't know I was going to say this until I did— "there's Winnie."

Will cleared his throat. "Yes, Winnie." His voice was amused. He looked me in the eye, and I looked back. "She broke up with me. I thought you might have heard by now."

"I hadn't heard it from the source, so I didn't put too much stock in the story."

"She said I wasn't a very good boyfriend."

"I doubt that. You always seemed attentive to me."

"Oh, it wasn't that. I'm a genius with birthdays, and I always do what I say I will. You know that. The thing was, she suspected I was in love with someone else."

I took a deep breath and raised my right eyebrow. "Scandalous," I managed to say.

Will's mother got home then—since Will had been sick, she was always buzzing around him.

"Ma, can I go to the Vineyard for Naomi's dad's wedding?" Will called out.

"Absolutely not."

"I didn't invite him," I called to her.

"I knew *you* wouldn't," Mrs. Landsman said. "But that son of mine."

On the ferry ride to the Vineyard, Dad and I sat in the middle of a long pewlike bench with roughly a million sweating people on it. Rosa was on the deck with Freddie and George. Dad has always gotten seasick on decks, so I was keeping him company in the cabin. It had occurred to me that this was the last time it would be me and him for a very long while. Maybe Rosa, Freddie, and George were thinking the same thing when they'd decided to stay outside.

The day was bright and wet, and my clothes were sticking to me. I was seriously considering abandoning Dad for the deck (last time alone be damned), which at least had the benefit of a breeze, when he asked me if I was looking forward to the wedding. I told him I was. I said how much I liked Rosa Rivera and all the sorts of things I knew it would make him happy to hear.

"You seem a little flushed, though," he said.

I said I was just hot.

It was noisy and crowded in the cabin, in other words not a great place to talk about serious things, but Dad persisted. "How's James?" Dad asked.

Truthfully, I hadn't thought of James at all. I hadn't had time—not with Dad's wedding and Will's sickness and *Will* and my photography and tennis and yearbook.

It was strange, really. A couple months ago, I had thought I couldn't live without him.

Apparently, I could.

That I could forget him so easily, more than the loss of James himself, made me melancholy, I guess. I wondered if Mom had felt that way about Dad when she met Nigel again. I wondered if my biological mother had felt that way about my biological father, and even about me when she'd had to give me up.

"I don't see him much," I said to Dad finally.

"It happens, baby." Dad nodded and patted me on the hand, and then he read my mind. "You forget all of it anyway. First, you forget everything you learned—the dates of the Hay-Herran Treaty and the Pythagorean theorem. You especially forget everything you didn't really learn, but just memorized the night before. You forget the names of all but one or two of your teachers, and eventually you'll forget those, too. You forget your junior year class schedule and where you used to sit and your best friend's home phone number and the lyrics to that song you must have played a million times. For me, it was something by Simon & Garfunkel. Who knows what it will be for you? And eventually, but slowly, oh so slowly, you forget your humiliations—even the ones that seemed indelible just fade away. You forget who was cool and who was not, who was pretty, smart, athletic, and not. Who went to a good college. Who threw the best parties. Who could get you pot. You forget all of them. Even the ones you said you loved, and even the ones you actually did. They're the last to go. And then once you've forgotten enough, you love someone else."

I must have started to cry because Dad held out his sleeve for me to wipe my eyes on, which I did. It wasn't anything in particular that Dad had said, but it was like he'd read my mind and put words to all the things that had been brewing inside me for so long. We were so much alike really.

I wanted to tell him how I was in love with Will, but it was Dad's weekend (and me not a particularly confessional sort of person under any circumstances) and maybe he already knew it anyway. Besides, it seemed silly after we'd just been talking about James. I didn't want to be the kind of girl who always needed to be in love with someone.

So all I said was "I'm really happy for you, Dad."

Rosa Rivera had no use for the color white—not in decorating and certainly not in weddings. "I am not young or a virgin," she had declared, "and I have already worn a white dress once. This time, I will wear red." The only white she wore on her wedding day was a white ribbon that she tied around her waist like an afterthought and the roses that she wore in her hair.

"But, Mama, aren't white roses bad luck?" George had asked her. Rosa Rivera said she didn't know and she didn't care to know.

She didn't much care what us bridesmaids wore either. "You girls wear the white if you like. You are young, and it will set me off nicely, I think?" It was a suggestion more than an order. (Then again, most everything Rosa Rivera said about anything sounded interrogative.) Freddie and George decided to honor their mother's request as she had made so few, and we wore three nonmatching white dresses. Dad followed the trend with a beige suit that he had bought the summer we had wandered Tuscany. He either didn't care to remember or just plain didn't care that my mother had picked it out for him. A footnote to the day might tell that story: suit picked out by ex-wife.

The week before the wedding, I had heard Dad speaking to the wedding officiant on the phone. "Hmmph," he said when he hung up, "they want me to decide between 'I will' and 'I do.' I didn't know there was even an option. Which do you prefer, kid?"

"Pretty much everybody says 'I do,' right?" I said.

Dad nodded. "That's what I thought."

"But then again, maybe 'I will' is nicer. It has the future in it. 'I do' just has the present."

"You make a good point there," Dad said. "How'd you get so smart?"

I shrugged. "Probably all that time conjugating verbs for French."

"Not to mention I've already said 'I do,' so maybe this time I should try something else."

They said their "I will's" by the beach at sunrise, both Rosa's and Dad's favorite time of day. Rosa was a rooster and Dad was a vampire, but somehow they managed to overlap for a couple of hours every morning.

I was happy for Dad, but I also felt like I was losing him. I was that baby in the typewriter case all over again. Maybe this was just life? One orphaning after the next. They should tell you when you're born: have a suitcase heart, be ready to travel.

I was feeling rather sorry for myself when Rosa threw her bouquet. I hadn't even noticed until the flowers were already heading my way. My instinct has always been to dive and catch, and this is what I did.

"You're next," said Freddie.

"Not so fast," Dad said. "She's only seventeen." He appealed to Rosa like a put-upon father in a sitcom. "Maybe you should throw that again?"

I threw the bouquet to my grandmother Rollie, who was sleeping in a beach chair. Rollie didn't like to have to get up before noon if she could help it. She woke when the bouquet hit her lap. "Oh crap, not again," she said. She had already been married four times, so she tossed the bouquet in the sand as if it were on fire.

"Does no one want my bouquet?" Rosa asked. Her tone seemed to be joking, but I detected some degree of offense.

I thought of that time I hadn't taken Rosa Rivera's scarf and what Dad had said. I didn't want her to have hurt feelings on her wedding day, so I retrieved the bouquet from the sand. "I do," I said. "I want it."

As we were walking back into the hotel for breakfast, Dad whispered in my ear, "Don't worry. I know what you meant to say was 'I will.' As in, in the future. In the distant, distant future." He winked at me conspiratorially, and I didn't feel like an orphan anymore.

• • •

"Who's Martha?" I whispered from the bathroom of the hotel room I was sharing with Rosa Rivera's two daughters, who were already asleep. I didn't have to say what I was talking about. It was eleven, and I hoped Will would be awake.

"Hold on," he said, "I'll look it up."

I heard him breathing lightly and the rapid clack of his fingers on the keyboard. "She was the mother and daughter of the white person who discovered the island. They had the same name, and they both died," Will reported. "The natives called it something else, of course."

"Stupid white people," I said.

"Good night, Chief."

"Night, Coach, and thanks," I said.

There was a pause where neither of us hung up the phone. It might have been five seconds; it might have been five minutes. I couldn't say for sure.

"How was the wedding?" he asked.

"I don't know. It all sort of blended together. You have to take a ferry to get here and I practically felt like an immigrant. I was the tired, the poor . . ." I whispered.

"The huddled masses yearning to breathe free . . ." he continued.

"Exactly. Rosa was pretty. Dad was so happy. I was presentable. It rained all last night, and the humidity made it so I didn't have to press my dress."

"Did you take pictures?"

"No. I thought about it, but it suddenly seemed like too much bother to take my camera out of my purse. There were other people taking pictures anyway."

"Why aren't you sleeping?" he asked.

"I can't. My iPod died this morning, and Freddie snores."

"When will you be back?"

"Around nine." Will offered to pick me up. I told him that he needed his rest.

"It's just a drive, not a marathon," he said.

"I'd like that," I said, "but Dad left his car at the airport, so I have to drive it home." Rosa and Dad were leaving from Boston for their honeymoon. They were going to Bali, one of the few places he and Mom hadn't *wandered*.

"Drive safely," he said.

"I will."

I felt brave in the darkness, lying on the cool tile floor of the hotel bathroom. "You know something stupid? I really missed you this whole weekend, Landsman. I've gotten used to seeing you every day."

He didn't say anything for a little while.

"I missed you, too," he said. "I wish I could have come."

Fifteen

WHEN I GOT BACK ON SUNDAY NIGHT, THERE WAS A minor yearbook crisis. The grandmother of the girl who was supposed to photograph graduation died, so she couldn't be at the ceremony Monday night. I had to go in her place.

I was taking crowd shots when I spotted Raina through my camera viewfinder. She was sitting with James's grandfather and a man who turned out to be James's dad. She was fiddling with her camera, and she must have seen me looking at her because at the same time that I took her picture, she took mine. We both lowered our cameras and exchanged a weary sort of smile.

The band started to play the graduation march, a song which I've always found seriously depressing. It's easy to imagine pallbearers carrying coffins to "Pomp and Circumstance," and even more so when it's performed by Tom Purdue's out-of-tune high school band. They should play something more cheerful. Something like "Higher

Ground" by Stevie Wonder. Or if it was serious, maybe "Bittersweet Symphony" by the Verve. Will would probably have a million better suggestions than any of mine.

I'd photographed two previous graduations, and they had all looked pretty much the same: same navy blue gowns, same hats, same auditorium. We practically could have used last year's pictures without anyone having been the wiser. It was a cheat anyway—the ones I was taking wouldn't get published until the next year's *Phoenix*.

After the ceremony, I heard Raina call my name. "Naomi, come pose for a picture!"

I turned around and there was James, of course. He looked tall in his cap and gown. I thought about waving and not going over, but it seemed impolite.

"James, put your arm around Naomi. Now smile, you two. It's a great day!"

Something happened with the camera, which was an old-fashioned film one with an enormous flash. James's dad said he wasn't sure if the picture had taken, would we mind posing again? We smiled a second time, and that time I'm pretty sure the picture took. James's dad said he would send me a copy, but no one ever did.

James looked at the yearbook camera, which was still hanging around my neck. He ran his finger across the lens cap and asked me if it was "the same camera." I nodded. James picked it up in his hand and tossed it shallowly in the air. "Hardy little bastard," he commented just before he caught it. It was true. That camera had withstood a lot. Gravity. A trip down a flight of stairs. It had lasted a whole school year. Longer than James's and my entire relationship, not to put too fine a point on it.

I raised the camera and took James's picture.

We shook hands. I congratulated him again.

He was just one of one hundred fifty seniors whose pictures needed taking, and I had to get back to work.

On the walk home I called Will. "*Songs for a High School Graduation*," I said. "You know, instead of 'Pomp and Circumstance.' Discuss."

" 'My Back Pages' by Bob Dylan," he said.

" 'Friends Forever,' Vitamin C," I suggested.

"Maybe a little cliché. 'Bittersweet Symphony' by the Verve. You know, they never made a dime off that song, 'cause of a dispute involving the sampling of the strings."

"I already thought of that one. That and 'Higher Ground' were the first two on my list."

"Red Hot Chili Peppers or Stevie Wonder?"

"The latter, but you could really use either, right?"

" 'Song I Wrote Myself in the Future.' John Wesley Harding."

"You used that one on my second or third mix tape," I reminded him. "I thought you didn't like to repeat."

"I don't," he conceded. "But the last time I used it, it wasn't a commentary on the educational system, so it's different. Also, 'Ghost World' by Aimee Mann."

"I don't know that one."

"You'd like it. I ought to play it for you sometime."

It went on like this for the whole walk home. It was dark out by now, and it was as if Will and I were alone in the universe.

" 'At Last.' Etta James."

"Clever."

" 'Teenage Spaceship' by Smog."

"Or 'Teenage Wasteland.' "

"It's actually called 'Baba O'Riley' after composer Terry Riley."

"I always forget that. But how about 'Race for the Prize,' the Flaming Lips?"

And then, up the path to my house.

". . . Bob Marley, is it? There're covers, too. Or is his the cover?"

Down the hallway.

"The tempo's probably a bit erratic for marching, Naomi . . ."

I stopped in the kitchen to get myself a glass of water.

". . . haven't been enough fast ones. You don't want to get bogged down in slow songs. Maybe Fatboy Slim's 'Praise You' or 'Road to Joy' by Bright Eyes?"

In my room.

"That Whitney Houston song they used to use for that ad with the kids in the Special Olympics. What the heck's it called?"

I was lying on my bed.

"I'm so tired," I said.

"That's not what it's called."

"No, I meant that I'm exhausted."

"Well, you ought to go to bed, Chief."

"I'm in bed, but I don't want to stop talking," I told him.

"Okay. When you've been silent for more than five minutes, I'll know to hang up. Your cell phone'll time out after thirty seconds anyway."

We kept naming songs . . .

" 'Me and Julio Down by the Schoolyard.' "

" 'The Only Living Boy in New York.' "

"Too elegiac?"

"That's what's good about it for a graduation, I think."

. . . until I was asleep.

Ten months and one or two lives later, I was back where I started: alone again at *The Phoenix* at around seven on a Wednesday. There's not much to do yearbook-wise for the couple of weeks after the books have been distributed. I was thinking how unnaturally quiet and lonely the office was without anyone in it when my phone rang. It was Will.

"Are you at the office?"

"Just locking up," I told him.

He said that maybe I could stop by later, and then he hung up quickly, uncharacteristically so.

When I got outside, Will was at the top of the stairs, grinning sweet and crooked, like a swung dash. It was the first time he'd been on campus for three weeks, and he looked thin, but much better than that day when I'd seen him at the hospital. Arguably, his pants on this day looked worse: they were plaid "old man" pants, probably borrowed from his grandpa. He was better off in school uniform pants. But what could you do? That was my Will.

"Hey there! Why didn't you come up to the office?" I called to him.

"The front door was locked, and you have my keys. I decided to wait for you here."

I jogged over to him. "To what do I owe this honor?"

"A long time ago, I used to go to school here. I even used to be the editor of the yearbook."

"Nope," I said, furrowing my brow. "Can't say I recall."

He offered me his arm. "I've heard these stairs can be troublesome," he said.

"I think I can make it down unassisted."

"Just take my arm, Chief. It's safer. Don't you think that between us we've had quite enough calamity for one school year? If you fell . . ."

I interrupted him. "I didn't fall. I dove."

"Fine. Have it your way. *Dove*. In either case, I don't think I could bear you forgetting me all over again." He turned me toward him, so that we were looking eye to eye. When he spoke, his voice was low. "Take my arm, Naomi. I'd offer to carry your books, but I doubt you'd let me."

I laughed at him and linked my arm through his. We were the exact same height, and his arm fit well in mine.

We walked slowly out to the parking lot, where Will's car was parked. I was mindful of Will's health, but also it was probably the nicest hour of the nicest day of the year. Seventy-three degrees, and the sun was just going down, and the air was thick with grass and a hint of sunblock and something in the distance, something sweet and delicious that I couldn't quite identify yet.

I don't remember who it was, but one of us finally said to the other, "Isn't it funny that all those months ago we flipped a coin so that we wouldn't have to take this very same walk?"

One or the other of us replied, "And now I wouldn't mind if it were even farther, if we could just go on like this forever."

For the longest time after that, neither of us said anything. I was unaccustomed to his silence, but I didn't mind it. I knew near everything about him, and he knew near everything about me, and all that made our quiet a kind of song.

The kind that you hum without even knowing what it is or why you're humming it.

The kind that you've always known.

acknowledgments

I am thankful:

For books and those who publish and champion them. (Especially my own books, of course—many thanks to Sarah Odedina, Jonathan Pecarsky, Dorian Karchmar, Janine O'Malley, and the good men and women of Farrar, Straus and Giroux.)

For readers and their teachers.

For my parents, who censored nothing, and for Hans Canosa, who is, among other things, the best reader a gal writer could want.

I tell you, this is a good life.